LAST SEEN WEARING

By the same author

A Vow of Silence

LAST SEEN WEARING

VERONICA BLACK

St. Martin's Press
New York

Library of Congress Cataloging-in-Publication Data

Black, Veronica.
    Last seen wearing / Veronica Black.
       p.   cm.
    "A Thomas Dunne book."
    ISBN 0-312-05888-8
    I. Title.
PR6052.L335L37   1991
823'.914—dc20   90-27489
                                                            CIP

First published in Great Britain by Robert Hale Limited.

First U.S. Edition: July 1991
10 9 8 7 6 5 4 3 2 1

One

Being a single parent wasn't the easiest job in the world, Joy thought for the tenth time that morning. In magazines and television programmes single mothers coped beautifully, always exquisitely groomed, perpetually good tempered, with a wisecrack ready when anything went wrong. In reality it wasn't like that at all, at least not in her own case. There were mornings when she barely had time to drag a comb through her hair, let alone summon a wisecrack.

She reminded herself that heroines in magazine stories didn't exist after the last page was closed and that the mothers on television turned into actresses and collected their money. They were not left to cope with a leaking faucet or a sudden stomach ache that meant more excuses to be made at the restaurant.

'You should have had her adopted,' Mrs Clark said about once a month. Mrs Clark was probably right. It was stupid to try to bring up a child alone when one had no husband, no family and no real qualifications for a well paid job.

Mrs Clark was wrong. Joy knew that in the better moments when Sally was tucked up in bed, her thumb in her mouth, a lock of yellow hair straying over her face. Sally was a pretty child. People turned round in the street to admire her. Sometimes they stopped and made comments.

'Such a gorgeous little girl. You and your husband must be very proud.' There had been a time when Joy had answered honestly. 'No husband. I'm a single mother.'

She no longer did that. People never waited around long enough to hear the rest of the story. She didn't think it would have made much difference if they had. It wasn't a very original one. A girl of eighteen under the illusion that the man she loved, loved her too. Words whispered in darkness that splintered in the light of day.

'Women always behave as if they never had any choice in the matter. You must have weighed up the consequences.'

Except that she hadn't. She had only loved. Only believed that the baby would anchor him to her side. It hadn't, of course. He had made vague promises about this year, next year, but they meant nothing at all. She had finally realised that when he hadn't even bothered to come and see her in the hospital. She had worn her best nightgown with the fluffy jacket she'd knitted, and sat, smiling bravely, while other visitors came and went and the chair by her bed remained empty. That was when she had known it was finally over, had never existed beyond the physical save in her own romantic imagination.

She hadn't asked him for child maintenance though the Social Worker had tried to persuade her. Probably that was stupid too because she could have done with it, but she shook her head. 'I'll manage,' she said and the look in her eyes belonged to someone older than nineteen. She had managed too, though there were moments when she still felt the old clutch of panic at her heart at the thought that she was the only relative Sally had. Just as Sally was the only relative she had.

At the back of her memory was the last conversation

with her parents. She had been fourteen then, at the age when going on holiday with one's parents was Endsville.

'How anyone can turn down the offer of a trip to Switzerland in favour of the local gymkhana I never will understand,' her mother had said ruefully. 'It's very nice of Eleanor to take you in for a couple of weeks.'

'I could have managed by myself,' the fourteen year old Joy had grumbled. 'I don't have to be looked after like a baby.'

Eleanor Prentice had been a neighbour, widowed and older than her own parents with no children of her own.

'Well, I hope you win a rosette or two anyway,' her father said.

She had sensed that he rather welcomed the idea of having her mother to himself for a change without a schoolgirl daughter in the background.

She had waved them off cheerfully and gone round to the local riding stables to sit on the wall and wish she could afford to buy Midnight instead of merely borrowing him for three-day events. And she had squashed down a feeling of irritation against her parents who could have postponed their trip if they'd really wanted to take her with them.

A few hours later word of the plane crash had come and her irritation had been swamped by a terrible aching tearlessness and the unfamiliar and dreadful rituals of mourning. There hadn't been a lot of money, only sufficient to put her through secretarial college, while the sale of the house paid her expenses while she lived with Eleanor Prentice who had offered to take her in. It hadn't been Eleanor's fault that her grades in school had dropped to rock bottom or that the Company in which Joy's small inheritance was invested went bankrupt. Eleanor had been very kind, if slightly alarmed to find herself with a teenager permanently in the house.

Joy was told so often that she wasn't a bother that she became convinced she was a terrible nuisance.

She'd grown out of her love affair with horses and opted out of college, taking a short typing course instead, and getting herself a job and a tiny apartment in the nearest town. When Eleanor had told her on one of her weekend visits that she had met an old boyfriend and was getting married and going to the States, Joy had made it plain she intended to stay in England and tried not to mind the relief on the older woman's face. She'd been going out with Hal then and she'd let it be understood, mainly because she herself believed it, that they would probably be getting married quite soon.

She hadn't written to Eleanor, now Mrs Baxter, about the baby. What was the sense in moaning about something that was her own fault anyway? That was how Hal saw it anyway, behaving as if the baby had only the remotest connection with him.

They had been willing to keep her place open at the office, but that would have meant leaving the baby with a sitter for most of the day. In the end she'd decided to move on to the next, larger town, away from well meant sympathy and find an evening job or some kind of work she could do at home.

The restaurant stayed open until midnight so she could make up a bed for Sally in the tiny room at the back where the waitresses left their coats. During the day she took what typing jobs she could though her speeds had never been wonderful.

The restaurant arrangement couldn't go on for ever. At three Sally didn't always drop off to sleep the moment her head touched the pillow. She was quite likely to climb out of her bunk and trot into the main dining room, in her pyjamas with the rabbits embroidered on them.

'If it became known that a child was sleeping on the

premises I'd lose my catering licence, I'm sure,' Mrs Clark had said several times recently. 'And Welfare wouldn't be happy.'

Joy wasn't too concerned about Welfare being happy. What mattered to her was that Sally was close enough to be heard if she cried out in her sleep and that the wages Joy took home weren't all being spent on a babysitter. But there were difficulties. Sally was already too heavy for Joy to carry comfortably to the bus stop, and it wasn't fair to wake up a little girl every midnight and expect her to walk to the bus, duffel coat bundled over her night clothes.

The Social Worker had come round regularly for the first few months after her birth. Joy had been managing on the last of her capital and the occasional typing assignment and she'd obviously been coping well. The tiny apartment was clean and there were no marks of neglect on the baby. Gradually the visits had ceased. There were too many ill-treated children and incompetent mothers in the sprawling town to waste time over nice, efficient Joy Prentice.

Nice, efficient Joy Prentice sat now in the living room of her apartment and queried whether a person's back could actually break in two. The apartment was cheap because it was on the fourth floor with the nearest supermarket a full mile away and a view from the small windows of the local cemetery. Not a desirable residence from the usual standpoint, but the building was in fair condition; a small corner shop provided basic groceries; and there were benches in the cemetery where she could sit while Sally played on the grass verge.

The room was clean. Joy felt sometimes as if she had embarked on the cleaning of the Forth Bridge though the entire apartment was poky, but Sally seemed to fill every space as if she were composed of air. Air, however, didn't spill cereal on the floor or crayon on the walls when Joy wasn't looking.

At the moment the cereal was mopped up and only faint traces of pink remained after a strenuous session with the scrubbing brush. The table was pushed against the wall to make room for the folding stroller, the cardboard box where Sally's toys were kept, the airing rack that wouldn't fit into the minute bathroom. Against the opposite wall was a sofa and two armchairs flanked a rug at each side of the electric fire. Gas would have been cheaper, but there was no gas in the building. Joy switched it on only in the coldest weather. One corner of the room contained sink, cooker and a refrigerator that groaned and whined when it needed defrosting which seemed to be every other day. Through a half open inner door could be glimpsed the bedroom with its single bed and the cot that was really too small for Sally now. There was a wardrobe that had been there when Joy arrived and a shelf on which she kept the toilet accessories that wouldn't fit into the bathroom.

The walls were off-white which meant they always looked slightly dismal and showed every fingermark. She had hung pink curtains at the windows and scattered some cushions about, but their gaiety struck a false note. It was all neat, compact and somewhat depressing. Sally was taking her nap, a habit she fortunately hadn't grown out of yet. She usually slept for a couple of hours in the early afternoon which gave Joy a chance to catch up on any typing she had to finish. Soon she would be sleeping less, Joy supposed, and the typing would have to be fitted in elsewhere. It wasn't fair on a child to be cooped up if the sun was shining. In another year there'd be a place for her in the local nursery school, but that would cost money too. Joy sighed, then mentally scolded herself. She was in a better position than many. She was completely independent and healthy and Sally was growing up into a charmer. She was also, a niggling inner voice reminded her, twenty-two years old with no prospects of meeting a man unless she bestirred herself to do something about it. The ones she had met since Hal had walked out of her life were either married already and therefore in her own code strictly off limits or considered her fair game because she'd been stupid enough to have a baby without getting the father to marry her. Sometimes she was glad she had no illusions left, but there were other times when she saw the years of loneliness stretching ahead of her like a long dark ribbon.

From the bedroom Sally called out. She had finished her nap which was a pity because Joy hadn't roused herself to get busy with the typing. Some author she'd never heard of wanted a fair copy of his novel made. She had meant to get it finished as quickly as possible so that she would get paid, but she'd sat too long thinking about her aching back and the evening's work ahead.

She went into the bedroom to stop Sally from toppling over the side bars. At three Sally was plump with a deceptively angelic face. Her hair was that rare shade of yellow that has in it no admixture of red or brown; her eyes were a clear blue tilted at the corners like her mother's eyes and there was little of her father in her at all which pleased Joy when she thought about it. Only the charm was there but at Sally's age it hadn't lost its quality of innocence.

Rescued from the top bar and set on her feet she grinned up at Joy and said in her 'bossy' voice, 'Walk now.'

Unless it was pouring with rain there was always a walk after Sally's nap. Her day was made up of small events and she liked them to take place in the right order. In the morning she helped mummy to clean the apartment though the help wasn't always appreciated.

Then they went to the shops and then they ate lunch and then there was the nap at which she always mildly protested more out of habit than anything else, because she always fell off to sleep. After the nap came the walk. Sometimes it was to the playground where there were swings and other children. Sometimes it was to the park where there were ducks. The walk to the park meant getting a bus for part of the way. At other times when mummy was tired the walk took them only as far as the end of the road where there were stones standing up on end with writing on them and grass and bunches of wilting flowers laid on some. Today, from the way mummy sighed as she set her down, it was obviously going to be the end of the road. 'Walk,' Joy agreed. She could see her own face reflected in the mirror over the shelf and experienced as always a momentary shock, a denial that the girl with the dark shadows under her eyes could be the girl who had confidently expected Hal to marry her. If he met her now he wouldn't look at her twice, she thought wryly. The late hours in the restaurant had stolen most of the colour from her cheeks and there was a wariness about her mouth. 'Right then,' she said, forcing briskness into her tone. 'Let's get your coat and shoes on.' She took pride in the way she dressed Sally, always buying the best she could afford and never skimping on well-fitting shoes. The woman at the corner shop said that Sally was the kind of child whom it paid to dress nicely and Joy had treasured the compliment.

'Are we going to the park?' Sally asked hopefully.

'Sweetheart,' Joy hesitated, not wanting to disappoint her but knowing the evening ahead would be filled with rushed orders and laden trays.

'The gardens,' Sally said, with a comical look of resignation on her face.

'We'll go to the park tomorrow,' Joy promised.

Sally was not a demanding child. It was as if she guessed that Joy did her best. She had never enquired why she didn't have a daddy but she mixed so seldom with other children that she probably hadn't thought about it yet. That question would come when she started going to nursery school. Joy hoped she would be able to answer it wisely.

The gardens, as Sally called the cemetery, was a pleasant oasis in the middle of decaying streets and Victorian houses split into separate apartments. Subsidence had tilted many of the stone and slate headstones sideways and there were too many weeds for the old fellow who trimmed the grass to conquer, but what sunshine there was lingered here and the high surrounding walls made it safe for a child to run about.

It was visible from the windows of the apartment, but to reach it entailed walking down the street and cutting up the alley between the adjoining backs of high, gaunt houses with paint peeling from the doors set in the walls and the strong smell of cats.

Today the wrought iron benches were all empty save for a man in a polo necked sweater and jeans who sat on one, scribbling busily in a notebook. The sun glinted on fair hair so like Hal's that for a moment Joy felt a leap of disquiet, but then the man glanced up and she had a glimpse of a blunt chinned, plain face without a trace of Hal's good looks. He gave her a casual, uninterested look and returned to his writing. Four years before, Joy thought irritably, he wouldn't have dismissed her so quickly. Then she had had a vitality that matched her name and the kind of gamine prettiness that glows into beauty when the right person is there.

'Simon wants to play ball,' Sally announced.

Simon was her invisible playmate, though Sally evidently saw him clearly. Her descriptions of him were so graphic that Joy sometimes imagined that if she turned her head swiftly she might catch sight of him too. Simon was taller than Sally, hated rice pudding, loved chips and ice cream, never bothered to take baths and had curly red hair. It was Simon who had spilt the cereal and crayoned on the wall. Joy supposed it was natural for children to make up companions when they hadn't any. During her own childhood she had been crazy about horses. She hadn't ridden since her parents' deaths.

'Just along the path then,' she cautioned.

Sally began rolling her red ball along the ground. Joy leaned back and closed her eyes, feeling the sunshine on her face drain away the tension. Tonight they'd be busy at the restaurant. There was going to be a twenty-first birthday party. She recalled her own coming-of-age with a wry grin. It had been the day that Sally had decided to run a temperature after her inoculations and Joy had spent the anniversary spooning antibiotics down a feverish and reluctant throat. When Sally had finally settled for the night she had opened the half bottle of wine she'd bought and toasted herself.

The sunshine on her closed lids was darkened by a shadow. She opened her eyes and looked up at the plain young man who stood on the path, regarding her gravely.

'This isn't an attempt to pick you up,' he said pleasantly. 'I'm just leaving and I can't help feeling this is a lonely spot for you to be sitting in.'

'Hardly anyone ever comes here,' Joy said.

'That's what I meant. Wouldn't you be better in a playground or park?'

'If I wasn't too tired to drag myself there,' Joy said. 'It really is quite safe, you know.'

'As long as you're sure.' He nodded pleasantly and began to walk away.

In surprise Joy said, 'You were genuinely concerned.'

'There are still a few of us around,' he paused to say.

'Sitting in graveyards,' Joy said. 'This isn't an attempt to pick you up, but why?'

'I'm tracing my family tree. The Bairds used to live round here so I came to do some tomb spotting. I believe I've found great-great-Aunt Eulalia Baird but I have to go back to the Records Office to check it out.'

'You're the heir to a missing fortune?'

'I'm afraid not.' When he smiled he was less plain. 'I'm over here from Toronto, trying to find out a little about my ancestors. I teach History so this is by way of being a busman's holiday. I'm Rory Baird, by the way.'

'Joy Prentice.'

His handshake was warm, firm and not unduly prolonged. 'Pretty name.' He hesitated, then went on, 'Would it be threatening a happy marriage if I asked you to have a cup of coffee with me?'

'No marriage at all,' Joy said. 'I'm not sure about the coffee though.'

'It would relieve my mind to know you were drinking a cup of coffee with me and not sitting here all by yourself.'

'Well, not exactly by myself –' Joy broke off, looking past him towards where Sally had been rolling her ball. The path was empty. 'Sally! Sally!' She raised her voice and after a moment Sally came running from behind a tall headstone at the far end, bouncing her ball as she came.

'You know you're not supposed to go out of sight,' Joy began scoldingly. 'I was talking to Simon's daddy,' Sally said with a cherubic smile.

'Simon is quite enough without having his relatives along too,' Joy said and, catching Rory's questioning look, said, 'Simon is Sally's playmate, the sort grown-ups can't see.'

'I had one called Fred,' he informed her.

'Fred?'

'Fred Pickle,' he said, and as she began to laugh, 'I swear it's true. I can't imagine where I got the name from. I have two older sisters so as a child I spent a lot of time by myself. Fred was great company but he hated school. After I'd been going for a few weeks he just faded away.'

'Sally starts nursery school next year. I'm hoping Simon will fade away too.'

'Bound to. Meanwhile if you're not sure about the coffee can I bribe Sally with ice-cream?'

'Yes,' said Sally, hearing the last word.

'You've both twisted my arm,' Joy said.

She felt suddenly light hearted. It was ages since anyone had asked her to have a coffee. Occasionally a customer in the restaurant tried to make a date, but she had almost forgotten what it was like to be invited out for a casual friendly cup of coffee. 'There's a place I noticed on the corner,' he said as they went towards the gate. It was a small café, with a brave blue awning, and an air of keeping up appearances in the midst of decay. Very occasionally Joy went there with Sally for a coffee and cake, simply to get out of the same four walls for half an hour.

Once seated, their order given, there was a brief silence. The silence of two strangers sizing each other up and trying to decide if they wanted to be friends. Between them Sally said,

'I sleep in a café.'

'Oh?' Rory's thick fair brows lifted slightly. 'With Simon?'

'I work in a restaurant at night,' Joy explained. 'The owner lets Sally bed down in the back room until I come off duty. I don't want to leave her with a baby sitter every night, and in my case they cost the earth.'

'You sound like a resourceful lady,' he said.

'I do try to be.' She made a little face at the wistfulness in her tone.

'I envy you,' he said unexpectedly. 'I'm not a parent myself but from my own experience of family life I know that children are worth having, worth fighting for.'

'You're not married?'

'Engaged once but it didn't work out,' he said cheerfully. 'I take it you –'

'There's just Sally and me,' Joy said.

'And Simon,' Sally said through a mouthful of wafer biscuit.

They both laughed. Laughter subtly altered the situation, Joy thought.

'How long are you over here searching for your ancestors?' she asked.

'Two months. It's a kind of sabbatical for me. I've a month to go,' he said.

She stifled an unwarranted and ridiculous pang of disappointment. 'I did the tourist trail first,' he said. 'Stratford-upon-Avon, Haworth, the Lakes. This last month is devoted to the ancestors.'

'Great-great-Aunt Eulalia?'

'And others.' He smiled at her across the table. He had nice blunt white teeth and his skin was tanned. 'When do you get off duty?'

'Not until midnight. Later tonight. There's a twenty-first birthday party and it's likely to run into overtime.'

'What's the name of the restaurant?'

'Sunset House – yes, I know it sounds like an old folks' home, but Mrs Clark, the owner, wanted something Hollywoodish.'

'Is it near here?'

'St Mary's Road – ten minutes on the bus.'

'Do they run after midnight?'

'Until two.' Seeing his expression she added, 'You don't have to start getting concerned again. The drivers know me and the bus stops at the top of the road.'

'And it's none of my business anyway?'

'It's very nice of you to be concerned,' she said.

'It would be nicer if you were plain and unattractive,' he said, 'but I'm hoping that you'll come out with me – Sally too if you're only free during the day.'

'I do typing at home but that's in my own time.'

'I thought I'd give my ancestors a rest for a day or two and explore London. When did you last go to the Zoo?'

'A century ago,' she said solemnly.

'Not tomorrow. You'll be too tired. The day after? If you tell me where you live I'll hire a car.'

'Sally and I are used to buses,' she demurred.

'Cars are more comfortable,' he said.

'Yes, they are,' Sally agreed.

'You see, you are outvoted.' He grinned at Sally who grinned back.

'Then thank you.' Joy capitulated. 'You see that block over there? Sally and I live in an apartment at the back. Fourth floor. We overlook the cemetery.'

'Jolly for you,' he commented.

'I'm not superstitious.' With a hint of the flirtatious manner she had almost forgotten she added, 'One meets very nice people there sometimes.'

'Simon likes zoos,' Sally said.

'I shall hire a car big enough for four,' he said gravely.

He had a pleasant face, Joy thought. Strong and honest. She couldn't picture him leaving the mother of his child alone in a hospital ward at visiting time.

Sally had finished her ice cream and was wriggling. Joy, glancing at her watch, was surprised to find how much time had passed. She would have to give Sally a rushed tea and then catch the bus.

'I'm due at work soon,' she apologised. 'Thanks for the coffee and ice cream. Sally?'

'Thank you,' Sally said politely, brightening as it became apparent the grown-ups were moving. She held out her hand to the invisible Simon and followed her mother and the man with blue eyes to the door.

'Don't work too hard,' Rory said and strode off, turning at the corner to wave. Waving back, Joy wondered if he really intended to keep the appointment. He hadn't fixed an exact time, but she hoped he would turn up if only for Sally's sake.

'For my own too,' she admonished herself as they walked home. 'I want to see him again, not for any romantic reason but as a friend.'

Sally didn't eat all her tea, being already stuffed with ice cream and Joy put the remains into the wheezing 'fridge. Mrs Clark would have provided a supper for Sally at the restaurant but Joy didn't want to take more advantage of her employer's generosity than was absolutely necessary. In any case it wasn't desirable for a three year old to get used to rich food.

'That man,' Sally declared as Joy was gathering her night clothes together, 'wasn't Simon's daddy.'

'Which man, sweetheart?' Joy wondered if it would be chilly enough for a siren suit.

'The zoo man what bought ice cream,' Sally said.

'Who bought – no, he isn't.'

'Simon's daddy is very old,' Sally said. 'About a hundred.'

'Heavens, that is old! Do you want to take your doll or your teddy?'

'Both,' Sally said after consideration.

'Darling, I've got enough to carry as it is,' Joy began.

'The teddy then,' Sally said obligingly.

'Right!' Joy zipped up the duffel bag in which she kept her daughter's things and sat the large teddy bear on top. She had a scant ten minutes in which to wash her face and apply her make up. She slipped a coat over the neat black dress into which she'd changed for work. It was still light and warm outside, but in the early hours of the morning it would be dank and chill. The interlude in the café had done her good, she reflected. Her back was no longer aching.

They caught the bus with no seconds to spare and squashed into the only available seat, with Sally like the meat in a sandwich between her mother and her teddy bear. From this position she beamed charmingly at an elderly gentleman who waggled his fingers amiably at her.

It was past six when they arrived at the Sunset and Marie, who had been looking anxiously through the square bay window of the dining room, hurried out to the entrance.

'Mrs Clark's in a mood,' she confided as Joy went down the corridor. 'The silver isn't the way she likes it and the butcher let her down.'

Marie had a whiplash thin figure, crinkled blonde hair, and a brow perpetually furrowed over the ills of the world and any possible disasters that might happen.

'I'll settle Sally and be with you,' Joy soothed.

The tiny room at the back next to the staff cloakroom contained a bunk bed and a cupboard. There were hooks on the wall for outdoor clothing. A window looked out into a narrow alley where the bins were. It wasn't the most salubrious outlook for a child, she knew, but Sally was accustomed to playing quietly with whatever toys she had brought with her until she fell asleep.

'One day you and I will have a house with an apple tree outside the window,' Joy promised as she undressed the little girl, 'and as you drop off to sleep nightingales will sing.'

'Will there be a peacock?' Sally enquired.

'A peacock? Where did you get that idea?' Joy gave her an amused look. These days Sally was always coming up with new words, new concepts. It made her more interesting company as she grew up. It was also a sign that she was ready to start school, to widen her horizons further.

'Simon's daddy has a peacock,' Sally said.

Odd that she should start talking about fathers suddenly. Joy wondered if the sight of her mother with a man had stirred some longing, some knowledge that she was different.

'Joy, do hurry up.' Marie put her crimped head round the door.

'On my way. I'll look in on you in a little while, sweetheart.' Joy kissed Sally who sat neatly in the bunk, the teddy bear on the pillow beside her. She looked cute enough to eat, Joy thought, blowing an extra kiss as she closed the door and sped up the passage to the main restaurant.

'It would be appreciated if you had arrived on time,' Mrs Clark said icily, coming from the kitchen. Her normally genial expression was disapproving.

'I'm sorry, Mrs Clark,' Joy began.

'The silver could do with an extra rub,' Mrs Clark said, cutting short any explanations.

'I'll see to it,' Joy said and hurried past.

There were other customers as well as the birthday guests. They had to be cosseted and not neglected in favour of the private party.

The Sunset had slightly chi-chi decorations but the food was good and the service fast. There were strategically placed shell ashtrays in the roped off smoking section, and tall stiff palms that suggested a thirties movies set. Joy went into the service pantry and made a start on the offending silver which looked clean enough already.

She slipped back to check on Sally at eight o'clock and found her dropping off to sleep, the teddy bear in the crook of her arm. She tucked her in and went out again quietly, hoping that the noise of the birthday celebrations wouldn't rouse her. There were two baize covered doors to insulate the little room from the main part of the building so there was every chance that she would sleep as soundly as usual.

The girl whose birthday it was had auburn hair, a snub nose and a young man who hung on every word she uttered as if it was a pearl. The parents were a weary looking, amicable couple who looked faintly overawed by the grandeur of the occasion.

The butcher might have let Mrs Clark down but the other tradesmen had surpassed themselves. As she carried in the trays of salmon in aspic and the magnificent iced cake Joy found herself hoping there would be left-overs. She and Marie could enjoy an impromptu midnight feast and there would be a box of goodies for Sally the following day. Mrs Clark was never stingy about left-overs.

She was threading her way graciously between the tables now, her good humour restored, her pink rinsed greying bun skewered with a long butterfly pin, pausing to enquire if everything was satisfactory, accepting each smiling affirmative as a personal compliment.

Darkness had mantled the city and beyond the radius of brilliance cast by the lights in the restaurant was a wall of gloom punctuated by the street lights further along. Outside cars drove past in a fairly steady stream, their headlights dipped, one or two slowing as their occupants debated whether or not to eat at the Sunset.

She found herself with a spare moment when it looked as if everybody had been served and there was a lull in the arrival of newcomers. She went over to a vacant corner table and straightened the cutlery.

Through the window she saw a car slow down to a crawl and mentally braced herself for more customers but almost immediately the car gathered speed and went round the corner.

'Miss Prentice, one moment if you please.' Mrs Clark had on her up-market voice. Joy turned her gaze from the window and went back to the birthday group.

'We have been invited most kindly to join in the toast,' Mrs Clark said, beaming at her. Joy stood with Marie, raising her glass of champagne as they all sang 'Happy Birthday' and the girl with auburn hair giggled and blushed. After that there was the cake to be cut and borne off to the kitchen to be sliced, the chef retaining a few slices as 'perks', and more champagne to be poured and a new customer to be accommodated. Her back began to ache again and her glance to stray towards the clock on the wall. Midnight beckoned.

'I'll check on Sally,' she murmured to Marie who nodded.

She debated with herself as she went down the corridor whether or not to wake her in preparation for the trip home or to carry her to the bus stop. Sleeping, Sally was a dead weight and there was also the duffel bag and the teddy bear. A drowsy Sally was generally cross, whining as she clung to her mother's hand.

The light in the tiny room was still on. Sally disliked the pitch dark and so the low voltage bulb was left on all evening.

The bed was empty. Joy blinked at it for a moment. Sally must have woken up and gone to the toilet. She had been quick to catch onto the habit of sitting on the toilet and was rarely wet even at night. And the staff toilet had a low seat and a foot pedal that the little girl could just about manage. The toilet next door was vacant however.

Joy stepped back into the other room, the first faint

flicker of alarm ruffling her composure. The alley? Had Sally gone out there? It wasn't likely, but she opened the back door, and looked out, calling softly.

There was no answer save the mewing of a night prowling cat somewhere beyond the wall. The outer door was a tall, narrow one, set into the brick wall. It was kept closed but not locked. In any case the latch was too high for Sally to reach.

Joy took a few paces into the cool night air and stopped, her eyes falling on the dim shape that sat limply on top of one of the covered bins.

Sally might have slipped out if she were in a particularly mischievous mood, but she could not have sat her teddy bear where it now sat, its back resting against the brick wall. The bins were too tall for her to reach.

Two

'It's important to keep calm,' Mrs Clark repeated for about the tenth time, her hands plucking nervously at the black silk of her skirt. 'She wandered off down the street.'

'She couldn't have reached the latch on the outer door,' Marie said.

'Perhaps it was left open and then blew shut. I'll ask Chef.' Mrs Clark departed kitchenwards with the obvious relief of someone who had a definite task to perform.

The customers had gone, unaware that anything untoward had taken place. From the moment that Joy had gone stumblingly into the restaurant to whisper that Sally was missing, Mrs Clark had been determined not to create a fuss that might damage her business. She had speeded the departure of the customers in a way that would have earned her a Commendation had she been in the Diplomatic Corps, had sent the kitchen staff in three different directions in case Sally had merely wandered out, had deputed Marie to search the inside of the building, and made Joy sit down with a shot of medicinal brandy.

'Try not to worry,' Marie said now, running her hand through her hair and looking round in a distracted fashion.

'Chef says he latched the door himself before six this evening,' Mrs Clark said, coming back into the dining room. 'I've telephoned for the police.'

The word sounded strange and unreal in Joy's ears. Police were uniformed figures who held up their hands to stop people jaywalking, or made pronouncements on television about the rise in rape convictions. They came with news of air crashes. She felt as if she had been sitting for hours in a kind of paralysis, her throat burning from the sips of brandy that Marie kept urging her to take. It hadn't been more than fifteen minutes and she couldn't recall what she had been thinking about while she sat here at the table in the window with stray crumbs from the birthday cake scattered over the tablecloth.

'There's a car stopping,' Marie said, looking through the window. 'Not a police car.'

'Ten to one someone has found her wandering and brought her back,' Mrs Clark said on a note of optimism, heading for the entrance.

It was Rory Baird. To Joy he had an unfamiliar look

like a stranger dimly remembered. He was halted by Mrs Clark's hand on his arm, and was evidently enquiring after her since his head indicated her from across the dining room.

It was like watching a silent film, Joy thought irrelevantly, his politely enquiring face becoming startled and then concerned as Mrs Clark whispered rapidly to him. He nodded and strode towards Joy, saying without preamble as he reached her side, 'I drove over to give you a lift home. What's this about Sally being missing?' Her reply sounded so coherent that she was vaguely astonished.

'Her bed was empty. The back door wasn't locked – it never is, but the door that leads out of the alley was latched. Her –' For the first time her voice faltered slightly. 'Her teddy bear was sitting on top of one of the bins. It's too high for her to reach.'

'Where's the police?' he asked.

'I called them when it became clear she wasn't on the premises,' Mrs Clark said virtuously.

'Here they are now.' Marie went to open the door again.

Outside the Panda car winked its reassuring light. The policeman looked very young and pinkly scrubbed like an actor playing the role of a policeman in a farce. At his side was a policewoman with hair the same shade of auburn as the birthday girl. The policeman had his notebook ready in his hand. He spoke briskly as though he intended to make sergeant as soon as possible. 'We've had a report of a missing child.' His accent was clipped, Police Academy. 'I'll need to get down the facts as quickly as possible so we can start searching at once. You'll be the child's mother?'

His gaze had fixed on Joy who sat, white as her apron, her fingers locked about the brandy glass. 'Yes, yes, I am.' She forced her fingers to unclench, to set the glass down quietly on the table.

'May I have your name?' His pen was at the ready.

'Joy Prentice.'

'And the child's name?'

'She's a little girl,' Joy said chokingly. 'Sally – Sally Prentice.'

'And she's – how old exactly?'

'Three years and four months.'

She had been born shortly after Easter when the shops were still full of chocolate eggs and fluffy bunnies. She had been tempted to name her Easter but she might have been teased later on.

'Is your husband here?'

'I'm a single parent.'

'We'd better have the father's name just for the record.'

The father? Was that what they called a man who made love to you and then complained that you hadn't been careful enough?

'If you have the name –?' the policeman said politely. The implication that she might not be sure of the identity stung her out of the curious lethargy that had descended upon her.

'His name is Hal Fenton,' she said, 'and I've not seen him since Sally was born.'

'He doesn't contribute to her support?'

'No. He's never seen her.'

'Do you have his address?'

'He went up north. I haven't seen him. If you're thinking he might have taken Sally you're wrong. He never took any interest.'

'You don't have his address?'

Joy shook her head. This was becoming like some peculiar dream. Sally was missing and they wanted to know where Hal was. 'The firm he worked for?' She dredged up the name from her memory and gave it.

'Can you describe your little girl?' the policewoman asked.

'Of course I can describe her,' Joy said. 'She's my child.'

'You don't have a photograph of her on you? A recent one?'

'I have her photograph taken on each birthday. I don't own a camera.'

'So the most recent photograph would be four months old?'

'It's at home,' she said dully.

'You don't live on the premises?'

'I only work here as a waitress in the evenings,' she explained.

'I'd better take your home address,' the policeman said.

She gave it, watching him make another neat entry in his notebook.

'You bring her to work with you?' The policewoman sounded faintly critical.

'She sleeps in a room at the back. I can keep an eye on her.' Her voice trailed away.

'Give me a description of Sally and after we've taken a look at the back room we'll go and collect that photograph of her,' the other said.

'She's small for her age,' Joy said. 'Small and plump. Pretty.'

'That's true,' Mrs Clark put in. 'Very pretty. Big blue eyes and fair curly hair.'

'Any distinguishing marks?' He was still writing busily.

'I don't think so.' Sally, plump and pink in the bath. "Simon doesn't want to get washed today, Mummy." 'No,' Joy said. 'No distinguishing marks.'

'What was she wearing?'

'Shortie pyjamas with rabbits embroidered on two pockets in the top.'

'Colour?'

'Pink – for heaven's sake, how many little girls are
running round in the middle of the night wearing shortie
pyjamas with rabbits embroidered on them?'

'It's for the record,' the policeman said soothingly.
'Was she wearing anything else?'

'A blue siren suit.' At their enquiring looks she stum-
bled on. 'I have to take her home when we close up here
and I try not to disturb her more than I can help. Usually,
if the evening gets chilly, I put on her siren suit. She kicks
off the blankets and I – I like to be sure she's warm.'

The policewoman went out, pulling down the blind
behind the door. 'She'll radio in what we have already.'
the policeman said. 'Take another sip of brandy.'

'I want to keep a clear head.'

Would that go down as 'Non-drinker' or 'Can't hold
her liquor'?

'We're under way,' the policewoman said, returning.

'Shall we go and see where she was sleeping now?' her
colleague enquired. 'Do you mind coming with us? You
can tell us if anything's out of place.'

Marie and Rory went too, with Mrs Clark bringing up
the rear. The room looked small and bleak. Joy found
herself looking at it through the eyes of a stranger, seeing
the bunk with its blanket, the dim light bulb, the little
window that looked into the narrow alley with the high
door and the big dustbins.

'Is anything missing?' the policewoman asked. My
child is missing, Joy wanted to scream at them. My
beautiful little girl is missing.

'The blanket's still there,' she said.

'The teddy bear?'

'It was on top of the middle bin outside.'

'And you brought it in?'

'It was cold in the alley,' she said idiotically. She
couldn't recall the actual physical sensation of picking up
the bear and putting it down on the bed.

'The door wasn't locked.' He opened it.

'Nobody ever comes into the alley,' she said miserably.

'What about the other door?' He indicated it.

'The back pantry door is kept locked,' Mrs Clark said, 'until the rubbish bags are put into the bins. Chef assures me it was locked tonight.'

'And the alley door was latched?' The policeman had produced a torch and stepped out into the yard, shining it round. He surveyed the narrow alley and then went over to the bins.

'Chef looked in all of them,' Mrs Clark said quickly. Joy was conscious of Rory's silent presence at her side.

'Nothing there as far as can be seen now,' the policeman said. He came back into the room, switching off the torch, closing the door gently.

'Her shoes are here,' Marie said suddenly, diving to the end of the bed.

'Don't touch them please, Miss.' The policeman looked at Joy. 'You didn't put her to bed in her shoes?'

'Of course I didn't put her to bed in her shoes,' Joy said loudly. 'I'm not completely stupid. She had a pair of socks on. Not shoes, socks. Why don't you start looking for her? Why are you asking so many silly questions?'

She stopped abruptly, pressing her lips tightly together. The policeman smiled in an embarrassed way and went out into the passage.

'He's gone to make further radio contact with the station,' the policewoman said. 'There's already an all-points call out.'

'I'm sorry.' Joy pushed back her hair. 'I feel so – I want something to be done.'

'I'm sure everything possible is being done, dear.' Mrs Clark had the voice of a woman who pays her taxes regularly and expects value for money.

'She probably wandered out,' Marie said. 'She woke up and wandered out and the door was open. Chef made a mistake.'

'It was closed when I went out into the alley,' Joy said angrily. 'She's too little to close it behind her.'

'The wind blew it shut?' Mrs Clark suggested.

'There isn't much wind and it wouldn't latch a door anyway,' Marie said.

'Was Sally in the habit of wandering?' the policewoman asked. Joy shook her head again.

'She was always with me,' she said. 'That's why I bring her to work, so that she isn't left with strangers. She never does wander.'

'We'll go and pick up that photograph now,' the policeman said, returning. They walked in ragged procession back down the corridor.

'I have a hire car,' Rory said, speaking for the first time. 'Miss Prentice and I can follow the police car.'

'When we've taken the names of those present on the premises this evening.' The policewoman took out a notebook. Turn and turn about. Tweedledum and Tweedledee. Joy drew a deep, gasping breath, erecting barricades against hysteria. 'Starting with you, sir?' The policewoman glanced at Rory. 'Rory Baird. I'm on holiday from Canada.'

'Do you have your passport on you, Mr Baird?' her colleague asked. Rory produced it for their inspection. 'Diana Clark,' Mrs Clark said. 'I can vouch for my staff.'

'We'll take their names anyway, just for the record. Miss −?'

'Marie Phillips,' Marie said.

'I sent Chef home,' Mrs Clark interposed. 'He used to make little cakes for Sally. He is terribly upset.'

Because he didn't think he would ever make cakes for her again? Joy pressed the back of her hand against her mouth. Marie brought her coat and bag, helped to untie the white apron she hadn't taken off.

'The duffel bag,' Joy said loudly.

'Bag?' The policeman looked at her.

'A small duffel bag with Sally's night-things in it. It wasn't hanging on the peg.'

'I'll check the room.' The policewoman vanished.

'You brought it with you?' the policeman asked.

'I always do.'

'No sign of any duffel bag,' the other announced. Perhaps Sally had left of her own accord after all, but she would have put on her shoes.

'Are there keys for the back door and the door into the staff room?' the policewoman was asking Mrs Clark.

'Yes, but they're never used.'

'With your permission we'll lock the room for tonight. One of our fingerprint boys will be round in the morning. If by any remote chance the little girl hasn't turned up by then,' he added a fraction too late.

Joy heard herself give a harsh dry sob.

'You did offer to give Miss Prentice a lift,' the policeman reminded Rory. He nodded, drawing Joy's hand through the crook of his arm. In the car he gave her a long, steady look. 'When you've given them the photograph I think you ought to call your doctor. He'll give you something to help you sleep – unless you have something?'

'I never take anything. I don't want to take anything now. I only want Sally back.'

'The British police are very thorough I'm told,' he said. 'Fasten your seat belt.'

She fumbled with it. It wouldn't do to be in the hospital after a car crash when they brought Sally home. They would, of course, bring her home.

She closed her eyes briefly. Perhaps when they reached the apartment it would be to find a small, woebegone figure clutching a duffel bag sitting on the doorstep. Please God, let Sally be sitting on the doorstep.

The street light glared on an empty porch. Behind them the police car drew up. Rory took the keys from her hand and opened the outer door.

'There's no lift, I'm afraid.' At that moment it seemed like her fault.

'Bit of a climb for you,' the policeman said as they mounted.

'It'd get your weight down, Ken,' the policewoman said.

Ken the Policeman. It sounded like a card from Happy Families, but the policeman there was called Mr Plod. Joy's mind was a ragbag of stray thoughts. The apartment was cold. She went over and switched on the electric fire.

'Is this the photograph?' The policeman had lifted it down from the shelf over the fire.

'You'll let me have it back?' She didn't want to look at it. If she looked at it she would break apart.

'As soon as we've had copies made. I'll nip to the station and then call back for my partner here.'

Policeman Ken went out with the photograph.

'Shall I make some tea?' the policewoman asked.

'Tea?' Joy stared at her blankly for a moment. 'I'm sorry but I can't – yes, of course, tea.'

'I'll make it,' Rory said. 'I'm handy in a kitchen.'

'You sound like the ideal man,' the policewoman said. 'My boyfriend can hardly recognise a tea towel. Now, while the tea's brewing, let's see if we've got anything to go on. When did you last check on Sally this evening?'

She must have taken off her coat though she couldn't remember it. She was seated in one of the armchairs by the electric fire and the policewoman sat opposite.

'During the evening – there was a lull in the service. About nine o'clock? Maybe a bit later, I don't recall – Marie would know because she held the fort for a couple of minutes while I looked in on Sally.'

'Did you notice if the alley door was open?'

Joy shook her head. 'I just looked in. Sally was – no, it was eight o'clock. I remember now. They had just started on the first course. Eight o'clock.'

'Was she asleep?'

Joy nodded again. Her head was beginning to ache. Rory was pouring tea, looking round for the sugar.

'In the little cupboard over the sink,' Joy told him.

'You haven't been here before?' The policewoman glanced at him.

'We only met today.' Joy wondered if she'd said the wrong thing.

The other's glance seemed to sharpen, but she said only, 'You're not old friends then?'

'We got talking,' Joy said. Rory had put too much sugar in the tea. For shock, she supposed. 'Must be lonely – just you and the little girl,' the policewoman said.

The implication being that she went about talking to strange men. Joy felt colour stain her white face. 'Mr Baird was looking up his ancestors in the cemetery,' she said. 'Sally and I were there, playing.' And what kind of a mother takes her child to play in a cemetery? She drank her over-sweet tea.

'What happens now?' Rory asked.

'With a good clear photograph and an all-points call out we're already on the job. If she did wander off she'll be picked up fairly quickly.'

'She doesn't wander,' Joy insisted. Sitting still was intolerable. She rose and began to pace in the confined space available. 'She's never done such a thing.'

'Can she put on her own shoes?'

'She's very competent for her age,' Joy said. 'She can almost dress herself and she chatters a lot. She's very friendly.'

But it was not a world in which friendly little girls could move safely. She stopped pacing and sat down again heavily, averting her gaze from the empty space where the photograph had stood.

'That'll be Ken now,' the policewoman said as feet sounded on the stairs. 'The main door isn't kept locked? That's poor security.'

'There's very little crime around here,' Joy said.

'No news yet.' He made it sound as if that was cause for celebration. 'Now all I need is a description of what was in the duffel bag.' The inevitable notebook was out.

'Her vest and pants, blouse, jeans.' She pressed her fingers against her forehead. 'Comb, toothbrush, toothpaste, a hand towel. That's all.'

'What about other relatives? Is there anyone you'd like us to contact?' the policewoman asked, draining her cup and rising.

'There's just Sally and me,' Joy said as she had said before.

'There isn't a friend you can call to stay with you?'

'I'll be staying over with Miss Prentice,' Rory said calmly.

'We'll be in touch.' The policeman had put his notebook away. 'Meanwhile if there's anything at all you remember, no matter what, come round to the station – you know Queen's Road? And try to get some rest.'

The two of them went out, Rory accompanying them onto the landing to exchange a few brief inaudible words. Joy stared at the empty space above the fireplace. There ought to have been logs crackling there instead of imitation flames flickering against a shiny chrome background.

'You don't have to stay ,' she said defensively when Rory came back in.

'I'll snooze on the couch,' he said. 'They may have news in an hour or two.'

'You don't believe that,' she accused. 'You think she's been taken. I think she's been taken.'

'If she has,' he said, 'the chances are that she hasn't been hurt.'

'How can anybody possibly know that?' She clenched her hands in her lap.

'Because the duffel bag was taken too. Whoever took the bag wanted her to have things to wear, but they didn't stop to put on her shoes. Perhaps they were afraid of waking her up.'

'And the teddy bear on the bin?'

'Perhaps they couldn't manage to carry everything and simply left it there.'

'They, they, they –' She gave a choking little laugh. 'Someone has my daughter. I don't care what was in their minds or why they took this or left that. I want Sally back.'

'Do you really never use sleeping pills?' he asked.

'Never. I'm a very together lady,' she said shakily.

'More tea?'

'Nothing. I ought to have looked in on her later, after eight. I always do, but we were busy last night. She could have gone any time between eight and midnight!'

'I don't think it helps to go round and round possibilities,' he said gently. 'Go and rest for a couple of hours Even if you don't sleep a rest will help.'

'I don't want to rest. I want to go out and look for Sally.'

'The police can do a better job than you can. You have to be here when they bring her back.' He had said 'when' not 'if'. She felt an irrational surge of hope.

'I'll lie down for a couple of hours,' she conceded. 'I might recall something – I can't think what – but something that will help.'

In the bedroom she slipped off her dress and pulled on her dressing gown. In the other room she could hear Rory turning off one of the bars of the electric fire. She ought to have offered him a blanket and a pillow, she thought, and stood for several minutes, trying to summon the energy to act the hostess, and then she lay down, pulling the quilt over herself, turning her eyes away from the empty cot. She would have to buy a proper bed when Sally came back. If Sally came back.

Sobs tore through her so violently that her body jerked in pain. Sally might not come back. Her parents had waved goodbye and never returned to say hello. Why should this be different?

If Rory came in and tried to comfort her she wouldn't be able to endure it. There was no movement beyond the door though he had surely heard the stifled sounds of grief. She turned her face into the pillow and wept more quietly, tears soaking the cotton, her ragged breathing slowing and steadying as exhaustion overcame her.

Cold, grey dawn roused her. For an instant as she opened her eyes she was happy. Then the events of the previous night rushed in on her, contracting her heart with pain. From the other room came a clinking sound. She got off the bed and opened the door. Rory, in shirt sleeves, was preparing coffee and obviously trying not to make a noise.

'I'm awake,' Joy said. 'I did actually sleep for a while.'

'Good.' His smile told her that he had heard the weeping but that he would never intrude upon her feelings without invitation. 'Coffee?'

'When I've taken a quick bath. I feel a mess.'

'I'll keep it hot. You wouldn't have a man's razor on the premises?'

'Sorry.'

'When we've had coffee,' he said, 'I'll drive back to the hotel to freshen up. I'll call in at the station on the way back. You'll be alright for an hour.'

He spoke as if he trusted in some inner strength she possessed which was apparent to him but not to herself.

'You don't have to –' Joy hesitated, changing it to, 'I was going to say this isn't your problem but the truth is that I'm glad you're here. I can't seem to function properly.'

'I intend staying around,' he said. 'We've a date to go to the Zoo, remember?'

'I keep trying to think who would have taken her,' Joy said, 'but there isn't anyone.'

'While I'm out why not make a list of all the people you and Sally know?' he suggested.

'That won't take long.'

'It would help in the process of elimination. And a list of the places where you take her. Of course it's entirely possible that she's stepping into a police car at this moment on her way home.'

He didn't really believe that, she could tell. After a moment he said. 'It really would help to make a couple of lists, you know. It's better than sitting here letting your imagination run riot.'

'It's only that she's never been away from me before,' Joy said over a painful lump in her throat. 'What did she do when she woke up in a strange place?'

The words 'or didn't wake up at all' were not spoken.

'I'll go and make myself respectable,' Rory said, shrugging on his jacket. He nodded in a genial fashion and went out without touching her. When the door had closed behind him she drew a long quivering breath. It would be easy to sit down and cry. It was more sensible to keep busy. More sensible to push the anguish beneath the surface and go on.

In the bathroom she faced a reflection with white face and swollen, dark-shadowed eyes. It would upset Sally terribly if she came home and found her mummy had been crying. When she came home. When! She ran a cold bath and stepped into it, discarding her clothes, feeling the sting of the icy water as a kind of penance.

She was zipping up her jeans when the doorbell rang. A swift glance in the mirror showed a little more colour in her face. Rory was at the door with a strange man. Thin, dark, middle-aged, looking as if he hadn't had a holiday in a long while. 'Detective Fuller, Miss Prentice. Your friend called in at the station so I accompanied him back.' He had a flat, slightly nasal voice and a quick, hard handshake.

'She's not been – found?' Standing aside to let them in, she tried to keep her own voice steady.

'Nothing yet, I'm afraid. Her description has been circulated to every police station and to the Press. It won't be just a handful of people searching for her. May I sit down?'

'Yes, of course. I'm sorry.' She gestured to an armchair and looked helplessly at the two cold cups of coffee on the table. 'I haven't started making the lists yet.'

'I suggested that Joy make a list of the people she knows and the places she takes her to,' Rory said.

'Good thinking.' Detective Fuller nodded approval.

'There are so few,' Joy said helplessly. Somewhere at the back of her head was a memory of the girl who had always coped so well. 'After Sally was born I lost touch with the people I used to know.'

'Including Sally's father?'

'I haven't seen Hal for over three years. I told them that last night.'

'I just came on duty,' Detective Fuller said. 'Our best bet is to go over it again. You may remember something you left out last night.'

'I didn't leave anything out.' She sat down in the other chair. 'It was like every other evening. I work as a waitress at the Sunset Restaurant six nights a week. It's closed on Sunday. I get there at six and I leave at midnight, a little after usually.'

'And you always take Sally?' Joy nodded.

'I feel safer,' she said, aware of the irony, 'having her with me. She sleeps in the back room and when I finish work I carry her to the bus. Occasionally she wakes up but on the whole she's a heavy sleeper. I know it's not an ideal arrangement.'

'It's amazing what children get used to. Very adaptable,' he said absently. 'There wouldn't be a cup of tea or coffee going, would there? I dashed out this morning.'

'I'll make it,' Rory said. 'Coffee OK?'

'It'll wake me up,' Detective Fuller said. His small, sparkling brown eyes swept the room like a laser beam.

'I haven't tidied up,' Joy said. 'I can't think about ordinary things.'

'Looks fine to me. Just you and the little one live here then?'

'Yes.' Intercepting his glance at Rory she added. 'Mr Baird stayed over to keep me company.'

'Very kind of him,' Detective Fuller said without expression. 'I take it you don't often have overnight guests then?'

'I never have them.' Joy caught the shrill note in her voice and stopped.

'No boy friends?' She shook her head.

'I have to ask,' he said apologetically. 'Sometimes boyfriends resent having a small child around the place.'

'No boy friends,' she said flatly.

'And during the day? What do you do with yourself during the day?'

'I look after Sally and I do freelance typing.'

'This is what you're typing now?' He had risen and moved to the small desk in the corner.

'I haven't started it yet,' she said. 'I meant to yesterday but Sally woke up early from her nap and I took her out.'

'The Case of the Paper Doll,' Detective Fuller said. 'John Lime is the author, I take it?'

'I belong to an Agency, I go there and if there's any work for me I bring it home. The Agency take a percentage.'

'And you do that in between looking after Sally?'

'Yes.' Joy, accepting a cup of coffee, gave him a puzzled look.

'You're in an unusual situation,' he said.

'Not really. There must be hundreds of working mothers without husbands in the city.'

'Most of them have family or friends.'

'Both my parents were only children,' she said tensely, 'and I was an only child. When I was fourteen they flew off for a holiday together, the first one they'd ever taken abroad, and they wanted me to go with them, but I was at the stage of being in love with horses and there was going to be a gymkhana, which is why I'm alive and they're both dead, because the plane crashed at take-off. I lived with a neighbour then until I was seventeen. She was a friend of the family but then she got married and moved to the States. I got myself a job in town and then I got involved with Hal and found out Sally was on the way. Hal didn't want to marry me, so I decided to start out fresh. I moved here, had Sally –'

'Did the father know where you were?'

'Yes, I let him know. He didn't bother to come and see me – us. Not once. I knew then that I didn't want to marry him and I didn't want any child support. Most of the people in the antenatal clinic tried to persuade me to give Sally up for adoption, but she was mine.'

'No regrets about keeping her?'

'None. I can't understand why you want to know –' Joy paused, her hand flying to her throat. 'You think I made it all up, is that it? You think I hid Sally somewhere or – I love Sally. I kept her because I wanted to keep her and I haven't regretted it, not for one minute.'

'Nobody's accusing you of anything,' he said mildly. 'We have to check every possibility as a matter of routine.'

'Then you can check on the fact that I was absent from the dining room for about two minutes when I checked on Sally at eight o'clock,' she said. 'After that I was serving until past midnight and then I went to get her ready to come home and –'

'The rest of the staff say they didn't have occasion to go to the back,' he put in. 'The kitchen window looks out into the alley, but the blind was drawn down. There isn't a blind on the window of the room where Sally sleeps.'

'There's a curtain,' Joy said, 'but Sally likes to lie and watch the moon come up over the wall and she likes the light left on too. She –'

'Could be seen by anyone entering the yard then,' he said.

'Nobody ever does. Usually Chef goes in and out of the yard a couple of times. He likes to throw out the rubbish as he goes along, but last night it was a cold buffet and –'

'It looks like a planned snatch, you see,' he said. 'Who knows she sleeps at the back with the door unlocked?'

'The staff at the restaurant.'

'Whoever took her had to know she was in that back room,' Detective Fuller said, gazing thoughtfully into the dregs of his coffee. 'Now the window can't be seen from the back road because of the high wall. Of course they might have taken a chance on finding the door unlocked or planned on getting through the window, but they'd have to know Sally was there first.'

'Have you noticed anyone following you recently?' Rory asked. He was leaning against the sink, his eyes moving from the detective to herself.

'I haven't noticed anyone following me period,' she said wryly. 'I don't know why anyone should. Sally and I

– we're just ordinary. Next year she's starting at nursery school and then I'll be able to work days at the restaurant and do some typing at night. Why would anyone want to follow us and then steal Sally? It doesn't make sense.'

'Not yet, but it will,' Detective Fuller said, beginning to rise. All his movements were neat and spare as if he were used to fitting into a small space. 'I'd better be getting back to find out if there've been any developments.'

'I can't sit here all day waiting,' Joy said tensely.

'Pity you've no phone.' He glanced round. 'I saw lines outside.'

'Some of the tenants have phones.'

'Then I'll pull a few strings and get one installed as an emergency measure. You don't have to sit in waiting. Those lists that Mr Baird advised you to make – you could call in with them later. Oh, and would you object to having your fingerprints taken?'

'No, of course not, but why?'

'The teddy bear. It'll have your prints and Sally's on it and there might be others, though it won't be so easy picking up a print from fabric, but the glass eyes – we might just get lucky.' He was on his way to the door, pausing to say, 'I take it you'll be staying around, sir?'

'Yes,' Rory said simply.

There was a strength in his voice that made her feel as if, without spelling it out, he had just made a commitment to her.

Three

It was the first time in her life that Joy had been in a police station. The scuffed green floor and the notices that made a tatty collage against off-white walls gave her a general impression of shoddiness. Walking in with Rory she was greeted by the policewoman who was standing by the desk chatting to the sergeant.

'Miss Prentice, good morning. I hope you managed to get some rest.' Her voice was so bright that it was obvious there wasn't any news. 'Come into the interview room. It's more comfortable.'

'Thank you.' Joy noticed a small brooch pinned to the other's shirt and added tentatively. 'Mavis?'

'Sounds like a parlour maid, doesn't it?' She made a little grimace as they went into a side room that was only marginally more cheerful.

Ken was there, flipping through the pages of his notebook. 'Nothing yet, I'm afraid,' he said by way of greeting. 'Of course it's early days.'

'I read somewhere that the first twenty-four hours after a disappearance are crucial,' Joy said.

'It isn't twenty-four hours yet,' he pointed out. It felt like long days and nights of misery.

'Good morning again,' Detective Fuller said, coming in. His nod towards the other two sent them out, Mavis turning at the door to flash an encouraging smile.

'Did you make out the lists?' Detective Fuller asked.

'They're not very helpful, I'm afraid.' Joy handed them over. 'I really have lost touch with the people I used to know. There's the Manager of the Typing

Agency, and the staff at the Sunset, and the lady at the corner shop – my doctor though Sally and I are both very healthy.'

'What about the neighbours?' he asked.

'People keep themselves to themselves,' she said.

He nodded. In the old days neighbourliness had been common when each family had a separate home, but now that they were crammed into apartments and bedsitters they guarded their privacy jealously.

'And that's where Sally and I go,' she said, seeing him turn his attention to the other list. 'The Typing Agency, the playground, the park, the supermarket, the corner shop, the cemetery.'

He read off the list. 'Has anyone tried to get into conversation recently?'

'Lots of people smile at her. She's very pretty and friendly, but nobody in particular – no, she's always with me.'

'And you and Mr Baird have only just met, you said?'

'Yesterday,' said Rory. 'and I really am exactly what I claim to be. A school teacher, living in Toronto, single, no criminal record, over here for a couple of months.'

'I'm wondering, you see,' Detective Fuller said, 'what ι tourist is doing in a cemetery.'

'Looking up my ancestors,' Rory told him. 'If you care to check you'll see that Eulalia Baird is buried in that graveyard and she happens to be my great-great-aunt.'

'But you weren't looking up your ancestors, were you?' He glanced at Joy.

'I already explained,' she said patiently. 'It's a quiet pleasant place and Sally can play there without any danger from traffic. I usually take a book or some knitting.'

'And Sally plays alone?'

'Oh, she has Simon,' Joy began.

'She plays with another child?'

'An imaginary one. You know how small children often have imaginary friends?'

'I've heard of such things,' Detective Fuller said, sounding as if he didn't approve.

'Simon has red hair and gets blamed for anything naughty that Sally does,' Joy said. 'She made him up.'

'Is she often naughty?'

'No, of course not.' Joy stared at him. 'What are you implying?'

'Nothing at all. I'm just trying to get a picture of the whole situation,' he said woodenly. 'So Sally is a good little girl who, like many children, invents a playmate. I believe they grow out of it when they start school. She hasn't ever run away before?'

'No, of course not! Why should she?' Her voice had risen. 'She's a happy, uncomplicated little girl and I want her back.'

'Everything possible is being done, Miss Prentice.' He leaned back slightly in his chair, twisting a pencil in his fingers. 'Those aren't mere words. When a child goes missing we swing into action. Now I'd like to go back to your apartment. An engineer is coming to install a telephone. You may get a call later. In fact I'm betting on it.'

'How would anybody know the number?' she asked.

'We'll broadcast it and then if anyone has taken Sally they'll know where to get in touch. You'll probably get a number of crank calls but we'll monitor them through the station.'

'You're talking about a ransom call.' Joy shook her head in disbelief. 'That simply isn't possible. I don't have any money at all except what I earn at the restaurant and from occasional typing jobs. If someone's been following me they'll know that.'

'It's worth a try,' he said placatingly.

'You want me to stay in to answer the telephone in

case someone asks me for a ransom they must already
know I can't pay? That's crazy.'

'This entire affair certainly has some unusual
features,' he said slowly. 'Whoever took her knew where
she was sleeping, took her and the duffel bag, changed
their minds about the bear. We have it for you by the
way. No more than two sets of prints and those not
clear. Obviously yours and Sally's. We can take your
prints now for elimination purposes. Then you can have
the toy.'

'Something for me to play with until my daughter
returns?' she asked bitterly as he struck the bell on the
table.

'We are doing our best, you know,' he said mildly. 'Mr
Baird, would you object to having your prints taken?
Also for elimination purposes.'

'No objection at all,' Rory said equably.

A policeman, not Ken, came in with the fingerprinting equipment. While the messy and vaguely humiliat-
ing process was under way someone came in with tea
and biscuits. Sipping her own, her fingers still damp
from the sponge she had used to wipe off the powder,
Joy thought wryly, 'The great British cure for all ills. A
nice cup of tea.'

'We've managed to contact Sally's father,' Detective
Fuller said when the fingerprinting equipment had
been removed. 'He's working in Manchester and
wanted to know if he ought to come down.'

'Why?' Joy asked sharply, colour flooding her face.

'You don't want to see him?'

'Not now, not ever.' She controlled her flash of
temper. 'He's never taken the slightest interest in her,
never even asked to see her. It's a bit late for him to play
the worried father.'

'I told him that I didn't consider his presence
necessary at this stage. Ah, we can let you have the bear

and the photograph now.' Mavis brought them in. Ken was hovering at the door. Joy wondered if they slept together. No, Mavis had mentioned a boyfriend. It wasn't important anyway. The photograph was in a large brown envelope. Wordlessly she handed it to Rory to check. The bear was in a plastic bag, its scuffed fur and woebegone little black eyes echoing her own mood. Tears beaded her lashes as she took it. Less than twenty-four hours since Sally had decided to take it to the Sunset with her.

'We'll get the phone fixed now and the number publicised,' Detective Fuller said. Outside the sun shone mockingly. She sat silently beside Rory in the car as they drove back. The hours were blurring together. She mentioned making lunch, but Rory set her to brewing tea while he went to the nearest take-away for sandwiches. Two men in overalls crawled about the floor drilling holes and stringing flex. Detective Fuller departed and Mavis and Ken arrived. They were beginning to seem like members of the family, she thought grimly. She had put the bear, still in its plastic bag, in the cot and left the photograph in the big brown envelope. There were some things she was not yet ready to touch or see. At some point Mavis suggested a nice lie down, and she went obediently, lying stiffly, remembering, of all things, the almost guilty sense of disappointment she had felt at not being able to compete in the gymkhana after her parents' deaths.

When she came out into the living room again the engineers had gone and an early edition of the evening paper was on the table. Under the heading, Have you seen this Child? was a faintly blurred reproduction of the photograph she had provided and a smaller paragraph beneath that.

'The police are anxious to trace Sally Prentice, 3 years

old, who disappeared from the Sunset Restaurant in St Mary's Road between eight p.m. and midnight last night. Sally was wearing a blue siren suit over pink pyjamas. She has blue eyes, fair curly hair and is of a friendly disposition. Anyone having any information of her whereabouts is asked to contact –'

She dropped the paper back on the table and went to sit down, pushing back her tangled hair.

'Do you really think that someone might ring?' She looked at the shiny, silent phone.

'Bound to,' Mavis said. 'Whether the calls will be of any help remains to be seen.'

Rory came over and sat on the arm of Joy's chair, not touching her. 'The number's available between six and ten in the evenings and ten and twelve in the mornings,' he said.

'When the phone does ring try and keep the caller talking for as long as possible so that we can get a trace on it,' Ken said. He sat the other side of the room by what looked like a duplicate receiver. There were headphones on his ears.

The first call came dead on six. Ken nodded in her direction. Her hand shook as she lifted the receiver. 'Miss Prentice?' It was a woman's voice, cultured and low.

'Speaking.' Joy said.

'I want you to know that God is punishing you for having sex with a filthy male animal,' the voice said. 'You submitted to the temptation of lust.'

'Did you take Sally?' Joy's voice cracked on the words.

'Not I, my dear, but you must now repent,' the voice said softly. 'The Almighty will not suffer the children of the flesh to live.'

Joy slammed down the receiver and burst into tears. 'Crank call,' said Ken, taking off the headphones and rubbing his ears. 'Whenever anything happens they crawl out of the woodwork.'

'I'm sorry.' She groped for the handkerchief that Rory was giving her. 'I just – how can people be so cruel? How can they?'

'It's a cruel world, honey,' Rory said. He had put his arm round her and she leaned against it, feeling the strength of his concern. Throughout the day he had said very little, had never intruded, but without him she would not have retained her fragile composure. The telephone rang again and Ken put back the headphones.

'Miss Prentice?' A female voice this time. One she knew. 'Miss Matlock.'

Joy mouthed Typing Agency for the benefit of the others. 'I won't tie the line up,' Miss Matlock said crisply, 'but if there's anything at all I can do don't hesitate to let me know.'

'Thank you, Miss Matlock. That's very kind,' Joy said numbly.

Miss Matlock rang off.

'Is that Sally's mother?' The next voice sounded young.

'Yes,' said Joy.

'My friends and I are holding a seance,' the voice said. 'We're going to try and contact her.'

'What for? She's not dead,' Joy said angrily and hung up abruptly.

'Try to keep even the cranks talking a little longer,' Ken advised. 'They might just give us a lead.'

'Sorry.' She attempted an apologetic smile.

There were more calls. A teenager, giving her name and address and offering to let Joy adopt her baby when it was born, several people who had seen Sally being pulled into a car, riding in the sidecar of a motor cycle, in a bus, in a cinema queue with a tramp; a clergyman rang to say that if she wished to post a reward he and his parishioners would help to raise the money; one man rang and proposed marriage. All the names given were carefully noted. By ten Sally was as tightly wound as a piano wire, her eyes black shadowed.

'We'll disconnect now and go back to check these out,' Ken said. 'you've had a nerve-racking evening, Miss Prentice, but tomorrow might bring something more useful.'

'How long do you keep the number operational?' Rory asked.

'About a week,' Ken told him.

'Why only a –?' Joy's mind supplied the answer to her unfinished question. If nothing was heard within a week the chances were that Sally would never be found.

'See you tomorrow then,' Mavis said. Her voice was still bright but her eyes were sad. Joy whirled abruptly and went into the bedroom. Her own eyes were burning, her hands shaking. All her tears were drying up in the fear that scorched her. Behind her, Rory said,

'I wish there was something practical I could do.'

'It isn't your problem,' she said dully. 'You stopped to talk to someone and landed yourself in a situation that isn't of your making. You don't have to stay. You don't have to be part of this at all. Sally isn't your child and I'm not your responsibility.'

'I'm making it my responsibility,' he said and put his hand lightly on her shoulder. In any other situation this was the moment when he would turn her round, tasting her mouth for the first time. To her horror she felt the insidious stirrings of desire. It wasn't possible that she could feel that when Sally was missing. It wasn't possible that some other emotion could whittle away at the edges of her grief. She moved away sharply and pushed back her hair.

'I appreciate it,' she said and thought how inadequate

the phrase sounded.

'One day you and Sally will look back at this time and you'll be telling her how you felt.' he said. 'Afterwards –'

'Is there going to be an afterwards?' she asked very low. 'It's nearly twenty-four hours and nobody's come up with anything.'

'Sooner or later somehing has to happen,' Rory said.

'Don't feed me with useless clichés,' she said wearily. 'Maybe nothing will happen. Children have disappeared before and never been found. The front page story gets relegated to page three and then the back page and then it's forgotten until another child goes missing and then someone tries to make a connection.'

'It's too soon to be thinking in those terms,' he said. 'Look, why don't you let me take you out for some supper? I've got the hired car so we can go somewhere and eat.'

'Someone might come with news while we're out.'

'Not if we call in at the police station on the way there and the way back to let them know where we are. Do you fancy any particular place?'

'Not the Sunset. I never go out so I don't – there's a wine bar near the supermarket. On Churchill Road.'

'Make yourself pretty and we'll go.' He went back into the living room, closing the door. Her first date since she'd been going with Hal, and she had no interest at all in looking pretty. Life had its ironies.

She did possess one good dress which she'd acquired on a rare impulse buy the previous summer and never had occasion to wear. Boat necked and classically simple with a slim skirt and flaring sleeves it was a subtle shade of amber that brought out the lights in her brown hair. Putting it on, slipping her feet into brown court shoes she was struck by the contrast between the outfit and her own wan and pallid appearance.

For the first time in ages she opened the box of

glittering eye make-up that Marie had given her for Christmas. The taupe and silvery grey enlarged and emphasised her eyes. The mask, she thought, applying blusher with a careful hand, looked convincing.

'Is this wine bar very elegant?' Rory asked when she walked into the living room. 'If so I'd better go back to the hotel and change.'

'You look fine,' she said truthfully. He had the aura of a man who can blend without fuss into any background. Already she felt as if she had known him for years. It was as if their relationship had been fuelled by the recent events, moving into a deeper level because of her anguish and his concern. When they reached the police station she sat tensely while he went inside, but he emerged after a few moments, shaking his head.

'No news yet,' he said, rejoining her in the car. 'Apparently a team of volunteers is out searching all the places where a child might have strayed. Now where's this wine bar?' She gave directions, her eyes turning constantly towards the streets through which they were driving. It was utterly ridiculous, but she kept praying she would see Sally trotting along the pavement.

The wine bar was discreetly lit and comfortable. At least the dim lights hid the ravages of tears. On each table a rose-scented candle induced a romantic mood.

'You ought to be here with someone else,' she said. 'All this is wasted on me.'

'We'll come here again when Sally's back and we can appreciate it more,' he said. 'Meanwhile, how about an omelette and a glass of white wine?'

'Anything. I don't feel like eating.'

'But you're going to be sensible.' He beckoned a hovering waitress and gave the order.

'Why? Why should I be?' she demanded. 'My child is snatched from her bed. I have to answer dozens of questions, to listen to a string of crank calls. Why should I be sensible? Don't I have the right to go to pieces?'

'If you think it'll help,' he said.

'No, of course it won't.' She drew a long breath. 'I'm being stupid. It's only that I go over and over it in my mind. If I'd looked in on her more often – if I hadn't taken her to work with me. If, if, and none of it is any use.'

'I can imagine.' His hand covered hers briefly and was withdrawn.

'This hasn't been a very pleasant holiday for you,' she said.

'The holiday isn't over yet. Meeting you has been a bonus,' he said, 'and everything will turn around as soon as Sally gets back.'

He paused as the waitress brought their order, and nodded approval as Joy picked up her fork and dug it into the fluffy yellow mass. The omelette had tiny slivers of mushrooms and peppers in it and was delicately spiced. It tasted like straw but she ate steadily.

'Afterwards,' Rory said, attacking his own portion, 'I'd like us to get to know each other better. I know it isn't the right time.'

'Right now,' she said, 'I haven't any feelings to spare.' But there had been that moment in the bedroom when her senses had responded. 'I can appreciate that,' he said. 'I'm happy you don't mind my staying around. You know I've been wondering whether or not it might be a good idea to get a private detective on the case. No aspersions on the police but they have to go by the rules and a private agent has more scope. If nothing happens in the next day or two it might be worth considering.'

'Private detectives cost money – and no, I won't borrow from you.' She saw the offer forming at the back of his eyes and held up her hand. 'I don't suppose history teachers get paid millionaire salaries.'

'It was only a thought.' He was silent for a moment, frowning. 'What I hate is feeling so damned helpless.'

'I know,' Joy said. 'I feel the same way – as if there's something I ought to be doing but I don't know what.'

'When you've done your morning stint of phone answering tomorrow would you like to go round to the places where you usually take Sally?'

'You think it might help?'

Her whole being cringed away from the pain such visits would involve. It would be like moving through the past with a little ghost at her side. 'Perhaps something might jog your memory. Someone who is usually there missing, or you might recall someone staring at you – Lord, I don't know.'

He ran his hand through his thick fair hair. When he was younger he must have had a cowlick, she thought, looking at the telltale wisp of hair, wanting suddenly to smooth it down.

'Anything will be better than sitting still,' she said at last. 'Answering the telephone is – I dread hearing nothing and I'm scared of hearing something.'

'Whoever took her must have wanted a child very badly. There's a ray of hope in that surely?'

'Because they'll treat her well?' Joy sighed and pushed her plate away. 'I keep telling myself that, but it doesn't really make much difference. There are children to be adopted. They don't have to steal my child.'

'That's an important point,' Rory said.

'What?' Joy looked at him.

'As you say, if someone wants a child badly enough they can adopt or foster. If they're not suitable adoptive parents they can steal any child wandering in a playground, waiting to be collected from school – children are vulnerable. So why do they make things difficult for themselves by taking a child who is always with her mother, who is only alone in the evening and then the chef could have pulled up the blind of the kitchen window or you could have looked in on her – why so much trouble?'

'They wanted Sally, not just any child.'

'And there has to be a reason. It's not for ransom. If they've been watching you so closely they'll know that you can't pay ransom. Are you sure Sally's father –'

'If Hal couldn't take the trouble to come and see her after she was born he's not likely to go to the trouble of kidnapping her,' she interrupted. 'To Hal small children are a nuisance, to be kept at a distance and certainly not to be coveted.'

'Then there has to be another reason.'

'I don't know of any,' Joy said. 'I don't know of any reason at all.'

'And worrying about it isn't going to help. Joy, I'm sorry. I hoped to take your mind off the situation for an hour, but my own mind won't let it go.'

'I like that in you,' she said in a low voice.

'Maybe we should try not to think about it at all. That way something may come.'

'If something doesn't come soon,' she said tightly, 'I won't be able to carry on.'

'Yes you will.' He took her hand, holding it tightly. 'You have a lot of courage inside you that you haven't even tapped yet. It took courage to have her and courage to keep her instead of giving her up for adoption.'

'It would have taken more courage to give her up,' she admitted. 'You're giving credit where it isn't due. I wanted Sally. It was as simple and selfish as that.'

'And you'll get her back.' He spoke with a certainty that heartened her though she was sure that he couldn't possibly know.

'I'd like to call in at the station on the way back,' she said, giving him an apologetic look as she finished her wine. 'I feel I'm using you as a convenience.'

'I'm happy to be one.'

He was beckoning the waitress for the bill. This was a man, Joy thought, who without fuss would always be sensitive to one's needs and desires. She frowned slightly, checking the thought. It was foolish to reach out towards the first person who seemed to offer an anchor.

Opening the car door for her he observed, 'Don't waste your energy feeling guilty because you can't respond to anything that isn't connected with Sally. When you have her with you again you'll feel quite different.'

'When', not 'if '. She held that in her mind as they drove to the police station. 'You want to come in with me?' He glanced at her.

She nodded, knowing again that he had guessed her reluctance to spend even a couple more minutes alone in the car. As they walked in Detective Fuller emerged from the interview room and nodded a greeting. 'Nothing yet, I'm afraid, Miss Prentice. We would come round immediately, you know.'

'I persuaded Joy to have some supper with me,' Rory said.

'Good idea. One has to carry on as normally as possible,' Detective Fuller said.

'What exactly is happening?' Joy asked. 'What's being done?'

'Quite a lot.' His voice held professional reassurance. 'Sally's picture and her description have been widely circulated. We've the phone link set up which may yet yield fruit. A team of volunteers has been combing empty buildings, car lots, alleys – everywhere a child might hide. My team is working in relays round the clock, checking on every bit of information that comes in. The hospitals have been checked –'

'Hospitals?' Joy heard her voice rise.

'Women who have lost a child during the last year,

women who have been suffering from nervous symptoms.' He had not mentioned any who had a history of child molestation but she felt faint and sick at the prospect.

'You are only checking on women?' Rory asked.

'We're checking on everything.' Detective Fuller said. 'Ninety percent of investigative work is checking and then rechecking. We'll find something useful.'

'I'm sure you're doing your best,' Joy said dully.

'If nothing comes up in the next couple of days we may consider a television appeal,' he said. 'I take it that you'd be willing to do that?' Joy nodded.

'Try to get a good night's sleep.' He nodded again and went back into the interview room.

'Would you think me very rude if I said I wanted to be by myself tonight?' Joy asked when they were back in the car.

'You're sure you'll be alright?' He glanced at her.

'Quite sure.' She spoke firmly, straightening her shoulders. 'I promise to try to sleep. Will you come in the morning?'

'Of course.'

She was grateful for his acceptance of her need to be alone. When they reached the apartment block he switched off the engine and turned, cupping her face in his hands. 'This isn't the right time or the right place to tell you how I'm beginning to feel about you,' he said. 'I only want you to know that when all this is over there'll be time for other emotions and meanwhile we'll see this through together. 'Night, Joy.'

His lips brushed her cheek lightly. For a moment she wanted to turn and cling to him, to beg him to stay, but she drew away, letting herself out of the car, locking her own dawning response in some part of herself she would release in a happier moment.

Hurrying up the stairs she was acutely conscious of

the unaccustomed lightness of her arms. This was the first time in three years that she hadn't had a sleepy Sally – the second time if one counted the previous night, but then Rory had been with her.

The apartment was unbearable. Letting herself in, staring round at the clutter of cups left from earlier in the day, at the disconnected telephone that would begin to ring again at ten in the morning, at the empty cot half-visible through the open door, she felt a sharp regret that she had sent Rory away. There might still be time to call him back. Turning towards the door she saw the white slip of paper lying on the floor. She hadn't noticed it on coming in. Bending, unfolding it, she read the straggling capitals.

'SALLY WANTS HER TEDDY BEAR.'

Four

She sat down limply in the nearest chair and stared at the message. Her heart was jerking violently and her hands were damp. Someone knew where she lived. Someone had crept up the stairs while she had been out with Rory and slid the piece of paper under the door. The images rising in her mind made her shiver.

She would have to go at once to the police station. There might be fingerprints, some way of telling who had left the note. If only she hadn't sent Rory away. She let herself out again, locked the door with shaking fingers, and ran down the stairs into the street. The neon lights, set too far away, made pools of honey on blackness. A wind, sharp and unseasonable, nipped her bare shoulders. She had not troubled to put on a coat and the neck of the dress she wore revealed her shoulders discreetly. It was not a dress to wear when one was alone in a deserted street around midnight.

She began to walk rapidly, still clutching the slip of paper. The heels of her court shoes made brisk tapping sounds on the asphalt. At the top of the road a cruising taxi slowed and stopped in response to her wave. 'The police station in Queen's Road.' She got into the back seat, her damp fingers slipping on the door handle.

'Are you alright, Miss?' The taxi driver turned in his seat to give her a worried look.

'Yes, quite alright. Please hurry.'

Perhaps he had thought she was a victim of rape. The number of rapes being reported had risen sharply in recent months. The authorities were more sympathetic now. Think of that, think of anything except that faceless figure creeping up the stairs.

'You sure you're alright, Miss?'

As she alighted, fumbling for change, the driver gave her another worried look.

'Fine. Truly. Thank you.'

She ran up the steps into the drab chamber with the notices and newspaper cuttings on the walls. Mavis was signing something at the desk. Clearly she was about to go off duty, but as she caught sight of Joy her expression changed. 'Miss Prentice, there really isn't any –'

'News. I know. I've had a note from the person who took Sally.' She handed over the page and leaned against the desk, her breath coming as fast as if she had been running.

'I'll get Detective Fuller.' The policewoman went rapidly into the interview room. Detective Fuller had an overcoat on. She wondered vaguely if he was preparing to go off duty too.

'Miss Prentice, come in and sit down.' He put his hand on her arm, guiding her in. The paper was in his hand. She sat down, watching him slip it into a plastic bag.

'Where and when did you get this, Miss Prentice?' His flat, nasal tones had the unexpected effect of calming her down somewhat.

'About ten minutes ago. Someone must have slipped it beneath the door while I was out. I didn't notice it when I first let myself in.'

'Run down to the lab. with this,' he told Mavis.' If anyone's there wake them up and tell them I want this checked – not in five minutes but immediately. Is Mr Baird with you?'

'He dropped me at the front door and went back to the hotel. I wanted to be alone.'

'And you went up alone to your apartment?'

'Yes. Nobody was about.'

Mavis had left the room. She hadn't said anything about just going off duty.

'I ought to have left a man,' he said, frowning. 'Trouble is we're all overstretched as it is. Shortage of manpower. We can't cover every eventuality.'

'I do understand that. My prints will be on the paper, I'm afraid. I picked it up without thinking.'

'They'll be eliminated. I doubt if there'll be any other prints on it. Our quarry is well aware of modern police methods.'

'Could it be a hoax?'

'It specifically mentions the bear,' he reminded her. 'We were very careful not to give out any information about that to the Press.'

'If Sally is really fretting for her teddy bear –'

'Miss Prentice, I don't want to put ideas into your head,' he said abruptly, 'but it is possible that whoever

took Sally is playing a sick joke on you, sending you this
to distress you. I hope it isn't so, but it's a possibility we
have to consider.' It wasn't one that had occurred to her.
She had made herself believe that whoever took Sally
had wanted a child to love. That someone would be
sadistic enough to deliver the note as a kind of sick joke
appalled her.

'What made you decide to be alone tonight?' he asked.

'You make it sound as if it's unusual,' she said. 'I'm
always alone except for Sally. Rory spent an uncomfort-
able night on my sofa last night and I reckoned he'd
appreciate a good night's sleep.'

'Wouldn't we all?' he said.

'He dropped me at the front door,' she repeated. 'I
went up alone.'

'How did you get here now?'

'I was lucky. There was a taxi. I don't see what –'

'You wouldn't mind printing out that sentence for
me, would you?' He was sliding pen and paper across
the table.

'No, of course – you think I wrote the note myself?
You think I sent Rory away and then – that is sick.'

'It would be,' he said woodenly. 'However we must
cover every possibility. If you don't mind –'

She rose and went to the table, bending to print the
message angrily.

'Doesn't look the same at all,' he commented.

'Did you think I wrote it myself?' she demanded.
'Took my own daughter away?'

'Sometimes people do things under stress because
they think we're not pulling our weight,' he said
vaguely. 'I didn't really think you wrote it. Ah!'

A small man in overalls had come in. 'Caught me just
as I was going to call it a day,' he said. 'Miss Prentice, we
met before. Bob Sykes, Fingerprint Department.'

'Yes, I remember,' she said, not remembering.

'What have you got for us, Bob?' Detective Fuller asked.

'Miss Prentice's prints are on the paper. Also Mavis's – and yours, sir.'

'Nothing else?'

'Pity.' said Bob Sykes. 'Every criminal knows to wear gloves these days.'

'Anything else you can tell us about it?' Detective Fuller asked.

'I check fingerprints. I'm not a graphologist.' He sounded a trifle sour. 'Fairly expensive writing paper. The letters are straggling but the pressure is even. In late middle age, well educated, under stress.'

'Man or woman?'

'Oh, I'd say man, undoubtedly, but you can get another opinion.'

'Anyone you know like that?' They were both looking at her.

'Nobody,' she said. 'Nobody at all.'

'We'll have it further checked,' Detective Fuller added. 'I think we ought to have that phone operational all the time. Not to the public but we'll have a line linking you to this station all the time. Then when he contacts you again –'

'You think he will?'

'Whatever his motives he's almost certain to. He will probably instruct you how to get the bear to Sally. I won't put anyone on watch. Might frighten him off. As soon as he makes contact, by another note, I imagine, then ring through to us immediately.'

'And then what?' she demanded.

'And then we have him,' he said grimly. 'I'll have a car take you home, Miss Prentice.'

'Surely he'd realise that I'd come straight to the police?'

'He might. He might take a chance that you'd keep quiet. I'm glad you didn't.'

'Will it make it easier to get Sally back?' she said tremulously. He glanced at Bob Sykes. 'It won't, will it?' She intercepted the glance. 'It will make it easier to arrest him but it won't bring Sally back.'

'In these cases,' Detective Fuller said at last, 'there are no guarantees.' Silently she went out to the waiting police car. The suspicion that she might have made things worse by coming here was harrowing. 'Would you like me to come with you?' The police driver glanced at her with the same sort of concern the taxi driver had shown.

'I'll be fine,' she said, forcing a smile. 'You must be ready to go off duty.'

'The wife always tells me that if she ever divorces me she'll cite the entire police force,' he returned, smiling. 'I'm always ready to put in a bit of overtime in a good cause. I hope you won't mind my saying this, Miss Prentice, but the way you're standing up to this – well, it commands our respect down at the station, it does indeed.'

'Thank you. Goodnight.'

Getting out of the car, walking up the stairs, she thought bitterly, 'That's me. Attagirl Joy. Bearing my illegitimate child without any backing from Hal, carving a place in the world for one small child and me, rushing about with my heart in my mouth and my emotions snarled like knitting wool. That's me.'

Entering the apartment she did what she had never done in her life before. She went into the bedroom, opened the wardrobe door, peered under the bed, glanced in the bathroom, stopped herself just in time from opening the refrigerator. Nobody but a dwarf could have hidden here anyway, or did she think Sally had been stolen away by the Little Folk who dance through children's dreams? She checked the door lock, put on the chain, wished she had invested in a spy hole so that she could check on visitors. She hadn't bothered because until now she had had no visitors

It was very late, the night hurrying towards morning. She took off her dress, forced herself to hang it neatly in the wardrobe, to wash her face and brush her teeth. The apartment was chilly but it would be more sensible to go to bed, to huddle within the cocoon of blankets and try to get warm.

She switched off the light in the living room and went over to the window to look down over the steep, shining black roofs to the paler shapes of headstones rearing up. Her parents were buried in the village cemetery where yew trees and an old manse made a picture postcard background to their mortality.

If the man contacted her again she would have to contact the police. She had promised. They would follow him and something would go wrong. She saw the hunched and faceless figure darting out into the street, alarmed by some suspicion that he was being watched. And a speeding car would knock him down. He would die without revealing where Sally was hidden. Locked in some cellar? In a box? Please God, not in a box!

Shuddering, she dragged the curtain across the window and went into the bedroom. The teddy bear lay still in its plastic bag, like something embalmed. She tore off the wrappings and held the furry animal close to her, wanting to cry but feeling the tears dammed up in her aching throat.

Drifting off to sleep she thought confusedly, Now I know why children sleep better with a cuddly toy. It is something to hold at bay the horrors of the mind.

Rory arrived at nine, his quick, concerned glance searching her face. She told him rapidly about the events of the previous night, breaking off to admit the engineers who came to install a direct line to the station.

'Did they get anything from the message?' Rory asked.

'It's probably an elderly man, educated, with an obsessive personality.' Her eyes were full of dread as she looked up at him. 'You know I've been hoping against hope that whoever took Sally was a young woman who wanted a little girl of her own to love. The police had that theory too, but an elderly man –'

'I ought to have insisted on staying last night,' he said moodily. 'You shouldn't have to go running through the streets at night.'

'From now on I'll have a phone link. Detective Fuller is sure he'll contact me again.'

'At least something has happened,' Rory said, echoing her own thought.

The engineers left; Ken and Mavis arrived in tandem. At ten the calls began. She found herself straining for the sound of an elderly male voice, but apart from a crank who whispered obscenities at her and might have been man or woman the callers were female, one or two offering to set up search parties in their area, a few feeling that they knew Sally from somewhere but they weren't sure where.

At midday Mrs Clark arrived with Marie in tow. Both of them, for some weird reason, had donned hats and gloves as if that were the correct costume in which to call upon a mother whose child has been kidnapped. The former carried a deep pie dish which she set with some ceremony on the table.

'Not wishing to intrude, dear, and the Lord knows I've plenty to be getting on with, but Chef sent these along for your freezer. You won't feel like cooking. Well, you do have a cosy little nest here, I must say.'

Her eyes hovered between Rory and the bedroom door. Some of Joy's gratitude evaporated.

'I've been going over and over it in my mind,' Marie said, 'but I can't think of anything out of the ordinary that happened the night before last. I mean you'd think that someone would have been loitering, wouldn't you? But there were only the customers coming in and the cars going past. Mind you –' She hesitated. 'It's probably nothing,' she resumed slowly, answering their questioning looks, 'but one car did go round a couple of times, slowed down too. I can remember that I thought at the time he was a bit slow deciding where to eat his dinner.'

'What sort of car?' Ken had removed his headphones and turned from the telephone.

'A big black one,' Marie said. 'Very posh.'

Joy's mind had clicked back. She could see herself standing at the restaurant window, see the big black car slowing down. That had been just before the birthday toasts were drunk. 'I saw it too,' she said slowly. 'About ten o'clock, I think.'

'Earlier than that,' said Marie. 'You were settling Sally down for the night. Just after six.'

'You say you saw it twice?' Ken asked her.

'About half an hour later. After that I was busy serving.'

'Could it have been the same car I saw later?' Joy asked him.

'You neither of you got the number?'

They shook their heads, Marie adding defensively, 'We'd no reason to.'

'You saw the driver?'

'I think he had a peaked cap on,' Marie said. 'Like a chauffeur.'

'I never saw who was driving,' Joy said. 'I was looking but not noticing.'

'Was anyone else in the car apart from the driver?'

'It was empty,' Marie said. 'That's what made me remember it.'

'You ought to have remembered it sooner,' Mrs Clark said scoldingly.

'It won't hurt to make a note and tell Detective Fuller,' Ken said, making a note himself.

'I do wish there was something I could do,' Marie said, her sharp little face gentling.

'Yes indeed,' Mrs Clark echoed. 'Sally was such a dear little girl.'

'Is,' Joy said harshly and looked down at the rug.

'I only meant –' Mrs Clark floundered badly. 'She's bound to be in a bad mood now, being kept away from her mummy and – well, chin up, dear. Marie, we ought not to intrude any longer.'

'We'll be back at six,' Mavis said, shrugging into her jacket. 'Remember you can phone out now directly to the station.'

'We're taking a drive out this afternoon,' Rory told them. 'Joy may remember something if we go to the places where she usually takes Sally.'

'Brave young woman,' Ken said, sounding embarrassed. When they had all gone, Ken continuing to question Marie about cars as they went down the stairs, the apartment enlarged itself again.

'I've never had so much company before,' Joy said with forced lightness.

'At least everybody's trying,' he said. 'Come on. You can show me where you and Sally go and that might provide us with a clue. You might recall something else, like that car slowing down.'

'I wish I'd taken a closer look at it,' Joy fretted. 'I just happened to be looking through the window when it slowed down and I mentally braced myself for another customer, but he went past. I wish I'd realised.'

'It probably had no connection. Where to first?'

'The playground and then the park. Those are two places I often take her.'

'Fine, and then we'll eat.'

Holding open the door he touched her shoulder

lightly, with a delicacy that made her feel cherished. The playground held its usual quota of small children, using the swings and slides, the brightly painted wooden roundabout. There seemed to be more mothers about than usual.

'We come and she has a swing. I push her,' Joy said, walking away from the car to the wire netting that surrounded the play area. 'Then she likes to go on the roundabout.'

'Is there anyone special she plays with?'

'We don't always come on the same day,' Joy said. 'She's friendly towards whichever other children happen to be here, but she hasn't any regular companions.'

'Have you ever noticed anyone hanging around?'

'I didn't look.' Her voice had sharpened as a small girl with fair hair went past, holding on to her mother's hand. 'I already told the police. Don't you start questioning me too.'

'How about some lunch?' he said equably.

'The park first. I'm sorry. I didn't mean to snap at you. I know you're trying to help and I'm being utterly stupid.'

'I think you're being utterly brave,' he said. 'Which way to the park?'

'Turn left at the bottom of the road and I'll direct you from there. Sally and I take a bus most of the way.' Turning her back on the gaudy roundabout, the swings and see-saw, banishing memories, she spoke calmly. 'It really isn't a long way but it's a bit far for her legs and she has too much dignity to agree to ride in a pushchair.'

'What do you do in the park?' He held open the car door.

'Play ball, feed the ducks, all the usual things.' She broke off, something brushing the edges of her mind as lightly as a feather.

'What is it?' Rory, now behind the wheel, glanced at

her.

'Nothing. I suddenly had the feeling that I ought to be remembering something, but I don't know what. Well, we feed the ducks, sail paper boats. Sally tells me that Simon loves to sail paper boats. Turn right here and then right again. The park's at the bottom of the incline.'

The park affected her less than the playground. There were fewer children here, more space. Rory parked the car and they walked, hands lightly clasped though she was not sure whether he had taken her hand or she had offered it. The sunlight glittering on the surface of the pond and breaking up the water into a million glittering droplets dazzled her eyes. She felt an irrational surge of hope. It wasn't possible that this ordeal would last for very much longer.

'The next time we come here there will be three of us,' he said and the way in which he picked up and gave expression to her own thoughts struck her afresh. 'Nothing comes to mind?' he asked after a few minutes.

'Nothing. I remember that I promised Sally I'd buy her a toy boat so that we could sail it here.'

'You, Sally and me.'

'And Simon.'

'Where did she get the idea of Simon from – the name, I mean,' Rory enquired.

'Oh, I told her once that if she'd been a little boy I'd have named her Simon. Now you're going to tell me she tried to provide me with a son.'

'Nothing so glib. I think she was providing herself with a companion of her own age, that's all.'

'If I'd been able to get her into a nursery school this year,' Joy said, 'she wouldn't have needed to invent him, or maybe she would. Rory, how can a little girl vanish from her bed without a single soul noticing anyone going into the alley? How can she stay missing after all

the enquiries that are going out? How can anyone dis-
appear into thin air and leave no trace? It's been nearly
two days and there is nothing. I begin to wonder if I'll
ever see her again. I begin to wonder if she's –'

He swung round, pulling her against him, kissing her
hard. For an instant the word she had been going to
speak hung on her lips and then she clung to him,
wanting to become part of his strength, part of his
certainty.

'Sally's fine,' he said, releasing her with a little shake. 'I
won't allow you to think anything else.'

'Sorry.' She summoned a smile. 'I think I'd like lunch
now.'

'I spotted a place on the way. Afterwards I suggest you
take a nap. You'll feel better after it.'

'Yes, Doctor,' she said meekly.

'It was a toss up at one time whether I'd be a teacher or
a doctor,' he told her. 'My dad's a teacher but my mother
rather fancied having all the family ailments treated for
free. As we're a fairly large family I reckoned I wouldn't
make much as a physician so I went in for teaching.'

She was astonished to find herself laughing. It seemed
unreal that she should be able to laugh when they still
hadn't found Sally. As her laughter died Rory said with
that quick sensitivity that made him less plain, 'Don't feel
guilty because something amuses you. Right now there's
every reason for us to hope.'

'No news is good news? I keep telling myself that.'

'It's usually true. Come and eat.'

They had lunch in a small restaurant and he talked
about the school where he taught history, about the
pupils who exasperated and enchanted him by turns. He
was thirty years old, his background was solid and stable.
Until now nothing dramatic had touched his life. He
knew exactly who he was, she thought, and reached out
to offer her his own certainties.

'Shall I come up with you?' Dropping her at the apartment block he glanced at her.

She hesitated, then shook her head. 'I want to tidy round before I take a nap. Will you come back at six?'

'See you then.' He raised a hand as he drove away.

The apartment smelt stale. She opened the windows, got out brushes and dusters. The mere action of cleaning made her feel as if she were doing something. Perhaps this evening someone would phone in with real solid information. Perhaps this evening Sally would come home. There had been occasions when she had wished she did have relatives who could give her a break by taking Sally for a couple of days. Thinking of those occasions now she felt a sharp pang and bit her lip, bending to polish the already pristine table.

She had run out of tea. The police force thrived on tea and coffee, she thought, making herself concentrate on practical matters. It was fortunate that she was well equipped with cups and saucers and mugs. For some reason she had bought several, with the notion in the back of her mind that one day her social life might blossom.

If she went to the corner shop she would have to face the well-meaning sympathy of the woman who ran it. Better to go to the supermarket where she was anonymous. She slipped a jacket over her blouse and jeans and added a headsquare, not because the weather required it but because she wanted to be merely someone in a crowd and not the mother whose child was missing.

A bus was just drawing up at the stop and she increased her pace to catch it. It was crowded with late afternoon shoppers and she strap hung, trying not to listen to the conversation between two women who sat near each other and communicated as if they were at a vast distance.

'And I said to her, "It isn't any use asking me for you were the last one had it, and if you use the eyes God gave you you'll see it on the telly next to Bert's photo." Kids!

'Wouldn't be without them though. That little one's still missing –'

'Probably murdered by now, poor little soul. They nearly always are.'

'Unless the mother did it. I was reading it's nearly always a relative.'

Struggling off the bus as it stopped she stood for a moment, fighting nausea. They were thoughtless women and what they said made no difference one way or the other, but it pierced her armour of calm.

The supermarket was across the road. She waited at the lights and crossed with a group of chattering schoolgirls. In their early teens, make-up inexpertly applied to faces still rounded in the plumpness of babyhood, their voices were light and happy. One of them, fair hair plaited into a ponytail, looked as Sally might look in ten or twelve years' time. If she doesn't come back, Joy thought with anguish, I might pass her by in the street and not recognise her.

She thrust the thought away and went into the supermarket, taking a wire basket, slightly disorientated by the neon-lit shelves with their plethora of goods. Sally adored supermarkets –

'Tea and coffee,' Joy muttered aloud and headed for the appropriate aisle. She added some biscuits to the load and a few bananas and went to the checkout counter.

'Would you be Miss Prentice?' The girl at the till gave her an enquiring look. For an instant Joy stiffened. No photograph of her had appeared in the newspaper but she did sometimes do her shopping here and it was possible the assistant had remembered her.

'Yes,' she said at last.

'There's a message for you. I was asked to hand it over.' She had produced a sealed white envelope.

'Where did you get this?' Joy asked sharply.

'Gentleman in a car gave it to me.' A lad stacking baskets at the side answered.

'When?'

'Five or ten minutes ago,' he said vaguely. 'I was wheeling the baskets into the forecourt.'

'What did he look like?' Joy clutched the envelope tightly.

'Didn't notice,' said the boy. 'He had a cap on.'

'And the car?'

'Big black one. Why?'

He had turned away indifferently without waiting for the answer. Joy paid for her purchases and went out, turning in the direction of the park. She couldn't bear to wait until she got home before she read the message. In the park there were benches. Seated on one she slid open the flap with her nail. There was a folded piece of paper inside. 'TOMORROW. BRING TEDDY BEAR TO CEMETERY. NO POLICE. TAKE HEED. NO POLICE.'

The same wavering yet strongly penned capitals. Each letter the same size. An obsessional personality. No police and that warning repeated for emphasis. She folded up the paper and slid it into the envelope. She knew exactly what she ought to do. She ought to tell Detective Fuller immediately as she had done before. He would have men stationed in the cemetery when she took the teddy bear there.

Whoever had given the message to the boy had followed her to the supermarket. He might even be watching her at this moment. Instinctively she glanced nervously at surrounding bushes and trees, at the gleam of the pond. Nothing stirred.

Whoever was watching her would know if she informed the police. There was no threat in the note as to what might happen to Sally if she did. The absence of a specific threat made it worse. It left her floundering, not knowing what to do for the best.

She had time in which to think about it. Stuffing the envelope into her bag she stood up and headed for the bus stop. She stood for a few minutes by the front door of the apartment block when she reached home, watching the stragglers coming along the road towards a lazy evening of television or whatever lucky people whose children weren't missing did to fill up their evenings. A sports car went past and a boy on a bike. Nothing else.

By the time everybody came back at six she was composed again, her eyes dark shadowed, her hair tied neatly back. Rory kissed her cheek as naturally as if he had been going out with her for months. Perhaps she would tell Rory. Perhaps not.

Detective Fuller arrived in between phone calls, accepting a cup of coffee from Joy, seating himself at the table. 'No leads yet,' he said without expression.

'You were told about the car?' Rory asked.

'I had a word with the other waitress, Marie,' he said. 'If you both saw the same car then it was driven round the restaurant at least three times. Probably checking the lie of the land. Tracing car and driver is another kettle of fish.'

The telephone rang again. Joy, assuring yet another well intentioned caller that she was in no need of spiritual guidance or financial help, rubbed the aching eyes wearily.

'I'm beginning to think the telephone ploy won't work,' Detective Fuller said morosely. 'Our quarry is too bright to be caught out by a tracer, and it's a big strain on you, Miss Prentice.'

'If it helps to find Sally –' she began wearily.

'I doubt that it will, Ken, take the calls for the rest of the evening,' he said brusquely. 'From now on I'll have all calls rerouted to the station. I'll leave you the direct line so you can get in touch. We're setting up an information room which ought to prove more useful.'

'Ought' and 'should' and 'might'.

'The truth is that nobody is getting anywhere, are they?' Joy asked. 'No leads, no clues, hours spent in listening to calls that don't help – it's a complete dead end.'

'We are doing our damndest,' Ken said, quietly reproachful.

'And it doesn't help.' She rose, moving to the window, looking out over the roofs to the quiet headstones.

'We'll fix up a television appeal,' Detective Fuller said. 'A personal appeal might bring us the break we need. Meanwhile if he gets in touch again –'

'Inform you at once. I know.' Her handbag was hanging by its short strap from the arm of a chair. She was careful not to look at it.

'When a child goes missing,' he went on, 'every man volunteers for extra duty. We do keep after the kidnapper, Miss Prentice.'

'For years,' Joy added mentally, and knew she wasn't going to tell anybody about the message.

Five

Rory had left her with a warm hug that stated more than it said. When they had all gone she put on the chain and drew the window curtains, feeling rather like a thief as she opened her handbag and took out the envelope. It and the paper were of the same thick, shiny quality, the ink very black – a fountain pen, she guessed. Her instructions were vague, no time being given, the spot where the bear was to be placed left unspecified. She wondered if there would be a further communication.

Tiredness was overwhelming her. She piled the cups and saucers in the sink, put the envelope back into her handbag, and went to bed, falling into an exhausted and dreamless sleep before she had time to weep.

It was after nine the following morning when she woke up. The initial feeling of optimism with which she greeted each new day was followed immediately by the shock of realisation. Sally was still missing. This morning the agony was blunted by the knowledge that at least something was happening.

She pulled on a dressing gown, decided the shadows beneath her eyes were fainter, and went into the living room to pull back the curtains and put on the coffee. She had just brewed it when the doorbell rang. That would be Rory. She felt a rush of pleasure as she went to unlock the door.

Her smile of anticipation faded as she saw the tall, good-looking man at the threshold.

'Long time no see.' Hal spoke lightly.

'What are you doing here?' she asked blankly.

'It's my child that's missing too.'

He stepped past her and looked round the room. She pushed the door closed with her foot and stared at him. Tall, broad-shouldered, muscles perhaps a little slack because Hal liked the good life, fair wavy hair, bright blue eyes. Well dressed, with an undeniable aura of success. An attractive, personable man.

'You've just remembered that you have a child, have you?' Bitterness welled up in her. 'For three years you ignore her existence and now you develop parental feelings?'

'Don't be sarcastic. It doesn't suit you,' he said. 'Believe it or not but I do feel a certain concern over the fact that she's missing. That's why I'm here.'

'If you wanted to express sympathy you could have sent a card.'

'You still feel badly about the affair, don't you?' He gave her a puzzled look. 'You ought to have had her adopted in the beginning.'

'I hardly think that you're in the best position to give advice,' Joy said coldly.

'You're right. I did behave badly.' Hal sat down and looked up at her. 'The truth is that I wasn't ready to be a husband let alone a father. I wasn't ready to make any firm commitments. You can understand that, can't you?'

'I never made any demands, financial or otherwise,' she reminded him.

'Very noble of you.' There was a faint sneer in his voice. 'Could that be because you only used me because you wanted a child for yourself?'

'That's a rotten thing to say.' She shivered in contempt, not only for him but for her own foolishness in ever having loved him. 'I told you about the baby. I waited for you to come but all I got was a note telling me you were going to work in Manchester.'

'I'd have supported you if you'd asked.'

'If I needed to ask then I didn't want anything. We've managed very well.'

'I'll grant you've done your best,' he said, 'but it isn't a marvellous best, is it? Our child sleeping at the back of a restaurant and being brought home at midnight?'

'This is only temporary.' Joy bit her lip and burst out angrily. 'I don't have to defend myself to you or explain my actions! I do the very best I can and you forfeited any rights you might have claimed three years ago. I don't know why you've come but I don't want you here. I don't want you here, Hal.'

'Not even for old times' sake?'

'Especially not for that. I'd like you to leave now if you don't mind.'

'You could at least offer me a cup of coffee,' he said placatingly. 'I've been driving since dawn. Your address was in the newspapers. I'm astonished not to see a crowd of sightseers.'

'If there have been then I haven't noticed. You can have a cup of coffee and then you can leave.'

Pouring it, adding sugar, she was annoyed to find that she remembered perfectly that he always took two spoonfuls.

'I really am concerned, you know,' he said. 'If it's a question of offering a reward –'

'It isn't.'

'Hear me out and don't jump down my throat. I'm doing well – very well – so if a reward for information is needed then I can help out.'

'It isn't needed, but thanks anyway. Here's your coffee. Remember the old saying? Black as night, hot as hell, sweet as loving? The perfect cup of coffee? I'm a bit more grown up than I used to be.'

'But still pretty,' he said softly. 'You were an attractive girl and now you're developing into a lovely woman.'

'Thanks,' she said shortly.

'The picture of Sally in the paper was a good likeness?'

'Very good. I had it taken on her last birthday.'

She fought against a sudden urge to weep.

'She looks a gorgeous child,' he said.

'That was the beautiful thing that came out of our relationship.'

'You don't hate me then?' He reached over and took her hand.

'No,' Joy said. There was faint surprise in her tone. 'I thought that I did, but the truth is that I don't feel anything for you at all.'

'Ouch!' He was still holding her hand and as she began to draw it away he pulled her closer, rising to his feet.

'Let me go, Hal.' Her face flushed as she tugged against him. 'I don't know what you've got in mind but I'm not playing games.'

'Neither am I.'

He had pulled her so close that she could feel his breath on her cheek. He was as handsome as he had ever been, his scent familiar. When he bent his head to kiss her she turned her head sharply and his lips grazed her cheek.

'Let me go, Hal,' she said flatly. 'It isn't any use.'

It was impossible to tell if he would have released her or not but they both heard the tap on the door at the same second. His grip slackened and he sat down as Rory pushed open the door and came in.

'Sorry I'm late but – oh, I'm sorry.' He had stopped, staring at Hal.

'This is –' Joy hesitated.

'I'm Sally's father,' Hal said easily. He had taken up his cup again and was sipping his coffee. 'I felt the least I could do was to come down and provide some moral support for Joy. This is a bad time for her.'

Rory's eyes flicked over the coffee cups, rested briefly

on Joy's flushed face and dressing gown and returned to Hal. There was a perceptible stiffening in his manner.

'Very bad,' he said. 'I'm Rory Baird, a friend of Joy's. I just dropped in to say that I called at the station but there still isn't any news. Detective Fuller says he'll be along later with the television people.'

'It's a relief to know Joy has good friends,' Hal said.

'Yes, well – I'll probably see you later, Joy.' Rory gave her a brief nod and went out again. It was only too clear what he must be thinking, she realised, closing the door and resisting the temptation to follow him down the stairs.

Hal's presence at what looked like a cosy breakfast, her own state of undress must have given him the impression that she was still on close terms with Sally's father. There was nothing she could do about it now without making things worse.

'You're going to be on television?' Hal enquired.

'They wanted me to record an appeal. I don't know if it will do any good.'

'You haven't talked to the newspapers yet?'

'I believe they were all asked to hold off for the time being.'

'When they do make an offer you'd better let me handle it.'

'What?' Joy stared at him.

'You can hold out for an Exclusive,' Hal said. 'The popular dailies might be prepared to bid quite high.'

'You think that I'd I'd sell my story to a newspaper?'

'They'll probably ask –'

'You think I'd make money out of the disappearance of my child? What kind of person thinks like that?'

'Someone with your best interests at heart,' Hal said.

In a moment she would fly at him, rake her nails across the smooth expanse of his well shaped cheek. She held herself very stiffly as she opened the door again and uttered one word, 'Out!'

'I was only weighing up the angles,' he protested.

'Yes, I can see that. That's all you ever do, isn't it? Weigh up the angles in every situation and see if there's likely to be anything in it for you. You never really cared about me or Sally. You never cared at all! Only for whether or not there might be any profit in it for you. Only for you.'

'I wouldn't take one penny,' he said.

'And you'd make sure that everybody knew you weren't taking one penny, wouldn't you? I'm not even blaming you because you can't help the way your mind works, but I don't want any part of it, not now or ever!'

She was white to the lips, her voice low and passionate. Hal had risen and was staring at her, his handsome face sulky. Why hadn't she noticed until now that Hal had a sulky face?

'OK. If that's the way you want to look at it I won't argue,' he said, lifting his hand in mock surrender. 'I'll take my advice elsewhere. You're wrong about one thing though. I did care about you very much at one time and I care about Sally's being kidnapped now. I'll see myself out.'

He had always insisted on having the last word. He was scarcely through the door when she slammed and locked it, then sat down in his vacated chair with her hands over her face, shaking from head to foot.

It wasn't entirely his fault. Slowly as her composure returned she told herself that. People couldn't help being true to their essential natures. Hal had always been an opportunist without any genuinely strong feelings for other people and he lacked the imagination to see how he appeared in his unrelenting selfishness. Their affair had been of the senses only, as light and insubstantial as the wings of a butterfly, and there was no point in expecting the wing of a butterfly to be made of steel. In one part of herself she could even feel pity for him because he might live out his life without experiencing one single honest emotion.

Rising, going into the bathroom, she ran a bath for herself. Not until she was scrubbed and clean, clad in fresh clothes, her hair combed, did she feel free of his touch.

She had just finished washing the cups when Detective Fuller arrived. 'Glad to see you keep the chain up when you answer the door,' he said by way of greeting. She thought it better that she didn't mention that generally she didn't bother, but that she didn't want to risk having Hal walk in if he decided to return.

'Is there any news?'

He shook his head. 'The usual calls. They're all being checked out. The television crew are coming this afternoon. They'll record a message from you to go out on the news. You don't have television?'

'When Sally is older I probably will get a set. I just didn't want her to get hooked too soon.'

'Well, you can either prepare a message or –'

'I just want to get her back,' Joy said tensely.

'Mr Baird not around?'

'Not at the moment.' Perhaps never again.

'Nice young man. Very sincere. I always fancied a trip to Canada myself.'

Joy wanted to smile and cry at the same time. Detective Fuller in the unlikely role of matchmaker. The pity of it was that by now Rory had probably convinced himself that she'd taken up with Hal again.

'I haven't been troubled by any reporters,' she said. 'I was afraid they'd be swarming round.'

'We requested them to hold right off. They've been very decent about it.'

'Sally's father was here,' she said abruptly.

'Down from Manchester?'

'Looking for an angle.'

'Perhaps he's concerned. Fathers do feel concern for their children –'

'Not this one.' Joy stopped.

'What is it?' His bright little eyes shot to her face.

'I'm not sure,' she said uncertainly. 'It's only that every now and then I get the oddest feeling that I'm on the verge of remembering something, something important. Then it slips away again and I lose it.'

'Something to do with Sally?'

'I don't know.' She shook her head. 'I honestly don't know. I'm sorry, Detective Fuller.'

'Not your fault,' he said easily. 'The human mind's a funny thing. Now I want to sit down with you and go over all your movements during the week that Sally was taken. I know we've been over and over it already, but I'll refresh your memory as we go along and you might just come up with something now. The black car for instance? Did you notice anything particular about it at the time? Was there something different about it that made you notice it in the first place?'

'My back was aching a bit,' she said. 'I was near the restaurant window and I saw it slow down. I recall thinking I'd have more customers to serve within a few minutes, but then it suddenly speeded up and went round the corner. After that was the birthday toast. The staff were invited to join in.'

'The driver of the car?'

'I can't recall even noticing him,' she confessed. 'I'm sure there weren't any passengers.'

'And you haven't noticed that car or any other car following you at any other time?'

'No, I'm sure nobody's been following me,' she said. 'Sorry, of course someone must have been following me – us, I just haven't noticed anyone.'

'And you never allow Sally out by herself?'

'She's three years old, for heaven's sake. She's never out of my sight.'

'Except when she's in bed at the restaurant.'

'And usually I look in every hour or so,' she said quickly. 'It was only that we were more run off our feet than usual that night.'

She could feel her composure cracking, and it was evident he heard it too since he rose, looking down at her.

'We'll leave it for the moment,' he said. 'If anything at all turns up don't forget you can ring through to the station directly. You haven't had any more messages?' She was thankful that at that moment her head was lowered and she was running her fingers through her hair for her expression would have betrayed her.

'About the teddy bear? No,' she said.

'Odd. I'd have sworn there'd be a follow-up,' Detective Fuller said. 'Of course our quarry might enjoy keeping us in suspense. The television crew will be here at three. I'll pop back then. Don't trouble to see me out, but don't forget to put the chain up after me.'

'Yes, of course.'

Staring at the door as he closed it behind him she thought that everybody in the world was coming to her apartment except the one small figure she wanted to see. Another who wasn't coming was Rory Baird. She was tempted to go to the hotel where he was staying and tell him that Hal meant nothing to her, but she quelled the urge.

If he had misunderstood then he must work the answer out for himself. She remembered with shame a certain letter she had once sent to Hal, begging him to reconsider his decision and marry him. He had rung up and told her that she was becoming a bit of a clinging bore. She had no intention of becoming a clinging bore again. Anyway she didn't owe Rory an explanation. She didn't owe anyone an explanation. If he decided not to come back then that was his responsibility. Having reached a firm and sensible conclusion she found herself crying again. It was as if she had lost not only Sally but the promise of something very precious.

She couldn't sit crying all morning. She pulled herself to her feet and began the task of cleaning the apartment save that when the bed had been made there wasn't anything to clean. No spilled cereal. No pink crayon marks on the walls. Lips trembling, she tried to think of something else.

She forced herself to eat some biscuits and a couple of bananas and then lay down, the questions that had been posed by Detective Fuller going round and round in her head. One day she would ask him a few.

Do you have any children, Detective Fuller? Have you ever snapped at one in a moment of exasperation and seen the trusting look falter for an instant and promptly knelt down and hugged the small offender? How do you feel about bringing back capital punishment for child killers, Detective Fuller?

The television crew arrived promptly and the apartment was suddenly a mess of cables and cameras and hand-held microphones. There seemed to be a crowd of people but there were no more than four, moving in and out, measuring distances, and using technical terms.

'The light isn't ideal,' someone said to her.

"I'm sorry. The next time my daughter is kidnapped I'll make sure the light is ideal." She was afraid she had said it aloud but she obviously hadn't because a bearded young man was talking to her.

'There really isn't anything to it. Just take your time and say what you want to say. If you fluff it we can always do it again.'

'I wasn't thinking of giving a theatrical performance,' she said lightly. He gave a faint, polite smile and turned to speak to Detective Fuller who had just arrived.

'Right, lights and positions everybody!' Someone clapped their hands and Joy found herself staring into the lens of a camera.

Someone snapped two boards together inches from her nose. She hadn't realised that actually happened. Someone ought to have given her a script. Meryl Streep would have made a better job of this.

'Ready when you are,' the bearded young man said encouragingly. For the flash of a second she froze, because it wasn't possible that she could be standing here, about to beg some unknown person to send Sally back to her. Then she raised her head and spoke steadily.

'My name is Joy Prentice and, as you probably know by now, my little girl, Sally, was taken away by somebody. I want to ask the person who took her away to send her back to me. She hasn't ever been away from me before, you see, and she's very little. Too little to understand. I miss her and I want her back. She's all I have. She really is all I have.' Her voice began to shake and she turned away.

'Fine. That's just fine,' the bearded young man said. 'Detective Fuller, if you'll position yourself here ready for a few questions?' Through the misery that engulfed her Joy could hear his flat nasal tones. 'Yes, one unusual feature is that the kidnapper has been in touch. I would like them to do so again. We are all waiting eagerly to hear.'

'Are you prepared to give any details about this communication, Detective Fuller?'

'Not at this stage, no, but if the person who did communicate will do so again we are ready to fix up a meeting anywhere, and agree to anything within reason to ensure Sally's safe return.'

'Does that mean you would be willing to offer a

ransom?'

'There's no question of that.' His tone had sharpened.
'I merely want to repeat that if whoever has Sally is
nervous about getting in touch, or if anyone suspects a
child is being held somewhere against their will every
call will be treated in the strictest confidence. Someone
somewhere has information about the whereabouts of
this little girl.'

'Would you like to repeat the description of Sally?' the
interviewer was inviting.

'She is small for her age but plump with curly fair hair
and blue eyes. A very pretty child.'

'I understand her photograph has been published
already?'

'Initially in the newspapers. It will be enlarged and
put outside police stations too during the course of the
day.'

'At the end of this news item we will be showing Sally's
picture on our screen,' the interviewer said. 'What was
Sally wearing when she disappeared?'

'A blue siren suit over a pair of pink pyjamas and
white socks.'

'Finally, Detective Fuller, do you have any theories as
to what might have happened to her?'

'We deal in facts not theories,' Detective Fuller said
stiffly. 'I can only repeat that if whoever is holding Sally
will come forward, contact us again, we will afford them
every consideration.'

Joy had had a vague idea of saying something that
might tell whoever might be watching the programme
that she hadn't told the police about the second
message. Now Detective Fuller was doing it for her
inadvertently.

'Lovely. That should bring a response,' the bearded
young man said. 'We're grateful to you. Miss Prentice,
thank you for your co-operation. I'm sure you'll have

good news soon.' He wasn't sure at all. He was just being kind, not saying what they must all be thinking. The longer a child was missing the less chance there was of finding her.

'Have you had a word with your doctor yet?' Detective Fuller came over to enquire. Joy shook her head. 'He might give you something to help you sleep.'

'I am sleeping, but I might go tomorrow.' It wasn't sleep she needed but Sally back.

'That's alright then.' He patted her shoulder awkwardly.

'Is there somewhere you can watch the item this evening?' the interviewer asked. 'We'll be putting it out during the news broadcasts today and probably tomorrow as well.'

'I don't particularly want to see it,' she said coldly. By the next day something else would have arisen to whet the public appetite for thrills, a starving child in some African country nobody had ever heard of, a Mafia godfather arrested, an earthquake at a safe distance.

They packed up their gear neatly and professionally and were suddenly gone. She had several hours to kill. Perhaps she ought to give 'him' the chance of giving her further instructions. There was a small cinema, already earmarked as a bingo hall, not too far distant. She decided to walk there, resisting the urge to glance over her shoulder every few steps.

The cinema was half empty. She took an aisle seat and fixed her gaze on the screen where huge images moved and spoke and emoted. She hadn't done this since Sally's birth either. It was a shame that she could not concentrate upon the film, could see only those printed words. TOMORROW NIGHT BRING TEDDY BEAR TO CEMETERY. NO POLICE. TAKE HEED. NO POLICE. The message burned in her brain. She hadn't told the police. Tonight she was going to the cemetery.

An elderly man shuffling down the aisle hesitated as he reached where she was sitting. She tensed, aware of him though she kept her eyes on the screen but he went on again. She had sat through the film without the slightest idea about the plot. When the lights went up she looked around but the cinema was less than half full and most of the patrons were couples.

Outside the darkness had arrived, clouds threatening rain later. She walked briskly back to the apartment. Earlier in the day she had hoped that Rory would come back. Now she hoped that he would stay away for a while.

The teddy bear lay on the cot, its fat arms and legs sticking up in the air. She picked it up and held it, unconsciously rocking to and fro as she considered a plan of action. She couldn't walk out of the apartment with it tucked under her arm. It would have to go into her canvas shopping bag which held it comfortably. She had no exact time when she had to deliver it which meant that someone would certainly be watching her when she went to the cemetery. There was still time to phone Detective Fuller.

She picked up the receiver, stood listening to the dialling tone, replaced it in the cradle and picked up the canvas shopping bag instead. The teddy bear was in the bedroom. She couldn't remember having put it down or come back into the living room. It was as if when the pain became too fierce part of her mind shut down and she operated on automatic pilot.

She pulled a jacket over her blouse and jeans and tied a headsquare under her chin. By now the television appeal would have gone out and she didn't want to be recognised by some casual passer-by. Inside she felt keyed up and shivery. Letting herself out of the apartment she wondered in what mood she would be turning homeward again.

At this hour the streets were fairly quiet. There were a few cars passing. She walked at a moderate pace, not glancing round, wondering if she were being watched.

She had never been to the cemetery after dusk and the possibility that the gates might be locked occurred to her as she approached and saw the iron bars gleaming under the lamp. By some oversight of the local Council there was an old fashioned street lamp jutting out here, its lantern more fitted to the grassy plots and yew trees than harsh neon would have been.

The gates were closed but not locked. She lifted the latch and stood, accustoming her eyes to the gloom, seeing the gravel paths stretching between the tall headstones. The bench where she usually sat while Sally played was by the wall. She walked steadily to it and took the bear out of the canvas bag. Out of the corner of her eye she thought she discerned a flicker, but it might have been only the wind stirring an errant branch. The headstones cast long shadows in which anyone might be standing.

'I brought this for Sally,' she said aloud and placed the teddy bear on the bench. Her nerves were wrought up to expect anything, but nothing happened. There were only the shadows and the silence marred by her own rapid breathing.

The flicker of motion was gone, if it had ever been. She risked a swift glance behind her, and then walked with equal steadiness back to the gate. Outside she leaned weakly against the wall. She would count to a hundred and then she would return. She closed her eyes like a good child at play and began to count slowly under her breath, her ears strained for any noise. On the gravel a footfall would sound like a pistol shot.

There was only the wind, moaning and twisting its way down the streets and alleys, bringing with it the first chill of autumn. She had lost count. Patiently she began again but her will was faltering.

Forty-three, forty-four – enough. She opened her eyes, turned and pushed open the gate again. Her feet made crackling noises as she walked rapidly down the gravel path to the bench. Towards the empty bench. The teddy bear had gone as if it had never been here. She had heard nothing.

'Are you still here?' She raised her voice. 'Where are you? Why are you doing this? What is it you want?'

No answer but at the other side of the wall a car started up. She whirled and ran back to the main gate, thrusting herself through the gap she had left, spurting to the corner where the surrounding walls bent at right angles. There was a narrow street here, with a fence confining its other side. She could see the tail lights of a car diminishing into the distance.

Fruitlessly she started to run after it but it was gathering speed, turning into the main road where it would quickly be lost in the mainstream of traffic. Sobbing, she slowed to a walk, her fists clenched impotently, the canvas bag dangling uselessly empty from her arm. A cat, streaking across the path, intent on a night's courting, brought her heart into her mouth.

She turned, feeling a stitch in her side as she hurried back, skirting the walls, turning into the alley that would being her back to the apartment block. Something moved by one of the old wooden doors that backed into the alley. Something larger than a cat, hands reaching, voice whining. 'Got a bob on yer, ducks?'

Only an old tramp, mouthing his plea auomatically, but she struck away the clutching hand and ran frantically, the canvas bag swinging wildly. The shape into which she cannoned held her tightly while she struggled in panic, the familiar voice demanding.

'Joy, what the devil are you doing out at this time?'

'Taking the teddy bear for Sally,' she said shakily.

'Someone scared me and I ran.'

'Taking the bear where?' Rory held her slightly away from him, looking into her face.

'There was another note,' she said. 'It was passed to me in the supermarket. It told me to take the bear tonight to the cemetery. Not to tell the police. Don't dare tell me that it was stupid of me to go. I know it was stupid, but if there was the slightest chance of getting Sally – I couldn't take the risk, don't you see? And you didn't come back. After this morning you didn't come back.'

'I've spent all day trying to make up my mind whether to come back or not,' he said, a faint grimness creeping into his voice. 'That scene with the girl in the dressing gown and a boyfriend who I thought was out of the picture – I played that scene with the girl I thought I was going to marry and I didn't want a repeat performance.'

'Hal turned up without warning, hoping there might be something in the situation for him to make capital out of. I thought he might be genuinely concerned about Sally. He wasn't.'

'No tender memories?' he asked wryly.

'None. He isn't a bad man, just shallow and selfish. He can't handle grown-up relationships, that's all. I sent him away.'

'And came trotting out all by yourself to deal with a kidnapper. You really do need looking after, don't you?'

'I put the bear on the bench where I usually sit,' she told him, 'and then I came away and waited. Rory, when I went back the teddy bear was gone.'

'We'd better go straight to the station – it looks as if the police are coming here.' They were nearing the apartment block and he broke off as a police car came down the road and drew up.

'It's Detective Fuller,' Joy said, not sure whether to be

glad or sorry as the detective alighted from the vehicle
and strode towards them, no friendliness in his voice or
manner as he said,

'Miss Prentice, would you like to come with me and
tell me exactly what game you think you're playing?'

Six

'The girl at the cash desk in the supermarket watched
television earlier and recognised you as the customer
she was asked to hand a message to. She assumed we'd
know all about it already but she got in touch anyway,'
Detective Fuller said, making no attempt to disguise the
annoyance in his tone. 'I take it you still have the note?'

She handed it to him silently. They were sitting in her
living room as if it were any other social occasion, but
she knew exactly what criminals felt like when they were
faced with arrest.

'I'll have it checked out for prints, but I doubt if any
will check with our quarry's,' he said, unfolding a plastic
bag and slipping the envelope inside. He had taken the
bag from an inside pocket and she found herself
wondering irrelevantly if he kept a supply of them
there. The police constable who accompanied him took
it. An older man than Ken, she had noticed, with an
expression on his face that suggested his bunions were
troubling him.

Detective Fuller's small searchlight eyes flashed back
to her. 'Why didn't you tell us about it?' he asked.

'I thought there might be a chance of getting Sally back – you don't have to tell me that I'm stupid. I know that. I also know there aren't any clues yet, and that scares me. The message told me twice not to go to the police.'

'The standard threat.' He permitted himself to sigh briefly.

'Well, what would you have done?' she questioned hotly. 'Staked out the cemetery? Don't you think he'd have been looking out for that? Alone I might have stood some chance – I don't know what, but something!'

'Too late now to cry over spilt milk,' he said, looking as if he wished he could. 'If you'd contacted me we'd have put a tracer bug inside the bear.'

'He must be watching me. He'd have seen you come.'

'There've been police in and out for days,' Rory reminded her.

Joy bit her lip and stared miserably at her shoes.

'You'd better tell me exactly what happened,' Detective Fuller said.

'I went to the cemetery at ten. He hadn't given a definite time so I picked ten.'

'We tried to ring you earlier but there was no answer.'

'I went to the cinema to give him the chance to pass me further instructions, but nobody came.'

'So you went to the cemetery at ten. Go on.'

'I did look around to see if I could glimpse anything, but I didn't want to frighten him off, so I put the teddy bear on the bench where I usually sit when I take Sally to play there and I went back through the gates.'

'Can you see that particular bench from the gate?'

'There's a big yew tree that obscures the view. Anyway I played fair.' She gave a dismal little smile. 'I closed my eyes and started counting to a hundred. I got about halfway –'

'Did you hear anything?'

'Only the wind. I went back inside before I finished counting because I was too jumpy to wait any longer. The teddy bear had gone. Then I heard a car starting up the other side of the wall, so I ran back to the gate and round the corner but it was too far ahead.'

'You didn't hear the car arrive?'

'No, I'm sure I didn't. The traffic noises are muted inside the walls but I'm sure I'd have heard one that was so close.'

'And you didn't get the number?'

'It was too far away, and it was too dark.' She lifted her eyes to his face. 'I really messed things up, didn't I?'

'As I said it's fruitless making a fuss about it now.' His weary glance moved to Rory. 'I take it that you weren't with Miss Prentice?'

'I turned up as she reached the apartment block.'

'Right then.' He nodded. 'I'll have the cemetery checked out, of course.'

'I can't understand how I didn't hear anything,' Joy said.

'The bear didn't run away by itself,' he said with sour humour. 'Someone legged it over the wall.'

'But surely the note was written by the same elderly man who wrote the first note,' Rory objected. 'That wall's high.'

'Then he's either an extremely active senior citizen or he has help.'

'Isn't the idea of two kidnappers far fetched?' Rory commented.

'You're right, Mr Baird.' The detective gave him an approving nod. 'Most kidnappers who are not interested with demanding ransom work alone. Often they act on impulse, snatching a baby from its pram or enticing an unescorted small child. This case has unusual features.'

She wanted to scream that it wasn't a case. It was Sally who had vanished and hadn't come home. As if he read her thoughts he glanced at her, saying in his dry, precise accents, 'I'm aware our attitude may seem to you to lack feeling, but we cannot afford to become emotionally involved. Gets in the way of common sense.'

'If that's all –?' Rory glanced at her too.

'For the moment. If you get any more notes, any communications from anywhere related to Sally, have the goodness to share them with us, will you, Miss Prentice? Believe me, but we do have the resources to deal with them.'

'Yes, I will.' She was on the point of apologising again but refrained. He was clearly anxious to get on with the job, unless he was going off duty to join a wife who must often feel annoyed at his unsociable hours.

'I'll see you out,' Rory said, making it clear that he personally wasn't going.

'Goodnight then.' Detective Fuller went, the constable following like a large sheepdog.

'He regards me as a complete and utter fool,' Joy said when Rory came back from the door.

'A somewhat abrasive personality,' Rory agreed. 'When did you last eat?'

'I can't remember.'

'The wine bar will still be open. Go and put on your pretty dress.'

'I'm not hungry and I'm not in the mood for pretty dresses.'

'I'm hungry,' he said implacably, 'and I want to see you looking your best.' For an instant she hated him, hated all of them with their insensitivity, their insistence that she go on living her life as if it had not been torn apart. Then she saw the concern in his eyes and gave in.

'Can you give me five minutes?'

'Take six,' he said with an almost jaunty relief. He was right to badger her into doing all the normal things, she admitted to herself as she changed into the dress she had worn previously. To keep going was important.

'You are the first woman I ever met who means six minutes when she says it, and performs wonders in that time. You look lovely,' he declared when she emerged from the bedroom. It wasn't true, she knew. Her eyes were still dark shadowed, her face was too pale even with blusher, but she was at least still functioning.

The wine bar was only half full. They went automatically to the table where they had sat on the previous occasion and, at an answering nod from her, he ordered the omelette and white wine again, but when the dish was set before her she gazed at it without interest.

'I truly am not hungry. I'm sorry, Rory.' She managed to speak lightly.

'Don't worry about it. I'll eat both portions,' he assured her. 'I always eat at moments of relief.'

'Relief?' she echoed, puzzled.

'I've spent the entire day wondering if you were going to get back together with Sally's father.'

'Hal is charming, handsome and irresponsible,' Joy said firmly. 'I don't think he knows the meaning of the word loyalty and he never does a good turn if there isn't anything in it for him, but I'm not sorry that I once had a relationship with him because it gave me Sally – Oh Rory, do you honestly believe she'll ever come home?'

The terror that gnawed at her had been expressed. She clasped her hands tightly together as she waited for his reply.

'I can only give you my theories,' he said, not insulting her with false comfort. 'I dare say the police have weighed them up already. But it does seem that Sally was taken because she is Sally. This isn't a case of a child being snatched at random from the streets. The man – and a man wrote the notes – wanted Sally, wanted her sufficiently to follow you both, to find out where she was sleeping, to take advantage of the back door being unlocked and to risk going in and taking her.'

'There's no reason why Sally was deliberately chosen,' Joy said. 'She's a lively, pretty child. I often hear people making admiring comments about her, but she's only really special to me. We've no money, no relatives. There isn't any reason.'

'Maybe not an obvious one but there has to be a reason,' Rory said.

'An elderly man.' Joy slid her untouched omelette across the table. 'An elderly man wrote the first note and probably the second one.'

'It was the same hand.'

'I think that Detective Fuller's right when he says a younger man probably took her. One of them is an obsessive man in late middle age. The other drives a big black car and shins over cemetery walls to collect teddy bears.'

'Perhaps the second one is a woman, and it was the elderly man driving the car. If they want her teddy bear then they must want to keep her happy, mustn't they?'

Her eyes implored him. 'Yes, I think they want Sally to be as contented as possible while she's with them,' he agreed.

'For how long do they mean to keep her?'

'I don't know, but my instincts tell me she's alright. If you can't eat then drink your wine and nibble a breadstick.' The order was like a caress.

'Hal wanted me to sell my story to the newspapers,' she said. 'That was when I ordered him out.'

'Would he stoop to kidnapping his own daughter in order to make some money?' She hesitated, picturing Hal. 'I'd have said no,' she said at last, 'but the truth is that the Hal I knew was just the invention of a romantic and rather silly nincompoop. He never really existed at all. I don't think he would but I don't know. Anyway he was in

Manchester.'

'The police checked that. I'd forgotten.'

'Hal was one of the first people they considered.'

'Perhaps he employed – no, that doesn't make any sense. If he could afford to hire men to kidnap her then he wouldn't have needed money in the first place.'

'Not to mention the fact that he knows I haven't any money.'

They stared at each other across the small table, linked in their bewildered anxiety. 'Do you think I'll be contacted again?'

'Let's hope so.' He pushed aside the second half-eaten omelette and smiled at her. 'Yes, he has to let you know where to pick up Sally.'

'I've been considering whether or not to go back to work,' she told him.

'Surely under the circumstances you're not expected.'

'No, but Mrs Clark will hold my job open for as long as is necessary, and I can't stand having nothing to do but sit in the apartment and worry about what's happened.'

'If it's a question of money –' He hesitated.

'That's not a pressing question yet,' she said quickly, 'but I need something to occupy my mind.'

'You do know that I'm staying around, don't you?' he said.

'Sympathy isn't love,' she said softly.

'Neither is gratitude,' he countered, 'but out of those emotions something will grow, if we give ourselves the chance.'

'If you're willing to take the risk.'

'The three of us.' He reached for her hands, holding them in his own broad, warm palms. 'Sally will come back, Joy. I said that I have an instinct about it and I'm not just saying that to comfort you. Until she does I'll be here –'

'You're due to go back to Canada,' she interrupted. 'You've a job, remember?'

'And three weeks vacation still to go. She'll be back before then.' She looked up to answer him and was momentarily blinded by a white flash.

'What the devil —?' Rory was on his feet but the man with the camera was already through the door. 'Detective Fuller said he'd asked the Press to hold off.'

She blinked away the dazzle. 'There's always the occasional bad apple.' Rory was still on his feet, staring at the glass panelled door. Outside a car started up and speeded away. 'I ought to have been quicker off the mark and grabbed his blasted camera.'

'And had a fight? That wouldn't have been very sensible of you.' Joy said. She was still trembling slightly but it did no good to dwell on the incident.

'I guess you're right.' He sat down again, reaching for his glass of wine. 'Let's drink a toast to Sally's safe return and then I'll drive you home.'

'To Sally's return,' she echoed.

'You're the lady whose little girl went missing?' The waitress, approaching as Rory nodded to her, looked sympathetic. 'I'm very sorry about the photographer. We don't encourage that sort of thing here.'

'It wasn't your fault.' Rory paid the bill.

'I hope she comes back soon,' the waitress said to Joy.

'Thank you.'

Going out to the car she reminded herself that most people were genuinely concerned, not out to make a profit. When they reached the apartment block Rory came up with her. 'I'm not inviting myself for the traditional nightcap.' He gave her a faintly teasing smile as they went in. 'I just want to make sure that nobody's hanging about.'

'And if there's another note,' she said, 'you'll be on hand to make sure I take it straight to the police. I really

do mean to keep my word to Detective Fuller, you
know.'

'I know,' He glanced about the room. 'There don't
seem to be any letters anyway.'

'You're thinking it isn't much of a place? Hal was
scathing about it.'

'I'm not Hal.' He hesitated for a moment, his eyes
searching her face. 'I have a small house in Toronto,
two bedrooms and a mortgage. But there's a garden at
the back. In winter the birds wheel and dip above the
snow, black on white, white against the black, with
scarlet holly berries to make kissing wreaths for
Christmas. You and Sally will like it there.'

At that moment everything was settled between them
and it felt right. Turning she went into his arms,
responding to his kiss with the last thought of Hal swept
clean from her mind.

'Do you want to stay?' She tipped back her head to
look at him.

'Yes, I do and no, I won't. When we spend he night
together it will be out of mutual delight to explore each
other with nothing to overshadow that,' he said.

'No nightcap then?'

'You're looking tired. Beautiful but tired.' He kissed
her again with a slow and sweet warmth. 'Why not sleep
in tomorrow?'

'I'll think about it.' Letting him out she was conscious
of both relief and disappointment. To have spent the
night together out of his desire and her lacking of
company would have been a mistake, but it would have
filled the empty space within her.

By now Sally would have the teddy bear – or would
she? The possibility that whoever had taken her was
now indulging in a sadistic game of Let's Pretend was
horrific. She had to trust Rory's calm certainty that Sally
was still alive, being held for some reason. Where? Was

she a long way away or closer than anybody realised? Joy had no instinct of her being near, no sense of her being anywhere at all.

She put the chain on the door and went wearily to bed. She was out of the habit of sleeping in. On the rare occasions that she did sleep through the alarm Sally was there, to climb out of the cot and tumble with her on the bed. 'Wake up, mummy, and get breakfast. Wake up, mummy.' Small fingers sought to lift her heavy eyelids, and a laughing little face rubbed iself against her own.

Joy sat up abruptly, rejecting the bitter-sweet lure of memory and went into the bathroom. She would make herself look as bright as possible and then persuade Mrs Clark that she was fit to return to work.

Rory hadn't arrived when she let herself out of the apartment and went to catch the bus. She debated whether or not to leave a note on the door, but decided there was no point in leaving what amounted to an open invitation to burglars. Not, she added wryly to herself as she sprinted for the bus, that she had anything worth stealing any more.

It was still early and there were only a few regular customers drinking morning coffee in the Sunset. Mrs Clark came forward at once, dignified in her black silk, taking Joy's hand as she said moistly, 'No news, dear? Well, they say that's a hopeful sign, don't they? Come into the back and have a coffee with me.'

The 'back' was not the small room where Sally slept but a slip of a parlour which Mrs Clark had appropriated as a private sanctuary. It was crowded as any Victorian chamber with a row of polished conch shells along the narrow window ledge, two velvet-backed chairs that would have suited dowagers and a round table inlaid with mother of pearl.

'Marie will bring us coffee,' Mrs Clark said as if she had a squadron of waitresses. In fact during the day she herself served with Marie and in the afternoons the Sunset was closed anyway.

Marie brought the coffee, embarrassing Joy by setting cup and saucer neatly before her with the deference she only displayed to customers. It made Joy feel as people must feel after a death in the family when other people walk round them on tiptoe.

'You seem to be bearing up,' Mrs Clark said.

'I was thinking that I might come back to work in a day or two,' Joy said.

'Surely you'd find that very difficult?' Mrs Clark sugared her coffee liberally.

'Not as difficult as sitting at home waiting for news. It would give me something to do.'

'If it's a question of money you are due for a small bonus.'

'It's not that, though obviously I'm going to have to start earning again,' Joy said. 'I simply want to get back into some kind of routine as quickly as possible. If you're afraid my mind won't be on my job then I promise that I'll try to – is anything wrong?' Mrs Clark had flushed, averting her eyes slightly.

'If it were up to me or the rest of the staff then there'd be no difficulty,' she said.

'But it is up to you,' Joy said.

'Well, not entirely, dear,' Mrs Clark said, taking a great interest in the silky surface of her coffee. 'One must consider the customers. The Sunset has always enjoyed a very high reputation. We get a very nice class of customer in here.'

'Reputation?' Joy stared at her in bewilderment. 'I don't understand.'

'Your coming back to work so soon might excite morbid curiosity,' the other said with a pained expression.

'Do you really think so?' Joy gave her a straight look.

'I can't afford to take the risk, dear,' Mrs Clark said.

'We've already had the police here and we've all had to make statements. I'm crossing my fingers that I don't get a warning from the Health Department on account of allowing Sally to sleep on the premises. Of course if she's found then that will make a difference.'

'Will it? I don't think so.' Anger coursed through her as she stood up. 'I won't take any more of your time, Mrs Clark. I'm very grateful for your past kindness.'

'If only you'd had her adopted in the first place,' Mrs Clark said unforgivably. Joy walked out, threading her way swiftly between the tables and chairs in the dining room, letting the glass door swing shut behind her as she went rapidly down the road. The sound of flying footsteps behind her halted her own. Marie reached her side, grasping her arm.

'What did the old cow say?' she demanded.

'Apparently I'm too infamous a character to be employed,' Joy said lightly. 'She seems to think that I might attract the wrong type of customer.'

'It's because of what was in the paper this morning,' Marie said.

'What was in the paper? Sally's disappearance isn't even front page news now.'

'You haven't seen it. Oh, well —' Marie had flushed scarlet. 'Look, I have to get back. I only wanted you to know that if there's anything at all I can do — are you alright for cash? I haven't got much but I can let you have a loan. Honestly she is so mean.'

'I'll be fine,' Joy said. The phrase was becoming automatic. 'Go back before you get into trouble.'

'If I didn't need it I'd tell her what to do about her old job,' Marie said darkly. 'See you.'

She fled back towards the restaurant. Joy walked on to the corner, pausing where a newspaper stand displayed its wares. The daily papers were ranged alongside various magazines. Her eyes were drawn almost compulsively to one of the less reputable papers.

The picture was very clear. She and Rory, hands clasped, looked up in startled surprise from the table on which two wine glasses and plates of food could clearly be seen. She handed over her money to the stall keeper and took the newspaper, folding it small and reading it as she walked along.

The caption accompanying the picture was vicious. 'Kidnap mother consoles herself.' The item beneath was stinging. 'Joy Prentice, unmarried mother of missing toddler Sally Prentice, took time off from helping police in their enquiries last night to sup with her close friend, Rory Baird. So far all investigations into Sally's disappearance have been futile.'

It was no wonder that Mrs Clark had refused to take her back. Had she read anything so damaging she might have hesitated herself – though she hoped she would have been less easily swayed.

She crumpled the paper into a ball and then changed her mind and headed for the bus stop. The police station was a hive of activity with bees in dark blue uniforms going in and out and the constant buzz of conversation. The desk sergeant was taking down notes from an agitated woman who was apparently complaining about her husband, thrusting a bruised cheek into the sergeant's face as she whined on. There was nobody about whom she knew. For a moment she hesitated, the bustle swirling about her, and then turned in the direction of the interview room.

'Sorry, Miss, but you can't go in there – oh, it's Miss Prentice, isn't it?' A policewoman, neat in her uniform, a sheaf of papers under her arm, had intercepted her.

'I need to speak to Detective Fuller,' said Joy tensely.

'He said you were to go straight in if you came. Not the interview room – his office.'

The young woman opened another door. 'Have you

seen this?' Joy went straight up to the desk where he was seated and smoothed out the newspaper, laying it before him.

'Of course.' He scarcely glanced at it. 'Cheap and snide. Do sit down.'

'Can't I do something? Get them to print a retraction?' She lowered herself unwillingly into the chair. The office was as bare and impersonal as the interview room without a single photograph or personal item to hint at the tastes of the man who now linked his fingers under his chin and gave her a long, considering look. 'A retraction of what?' he enquired. 'There's nothing printed there that isn't true.'

'But it makes it look as if I'm a completely uncaring mother,' she protested.

'You were in the wine bar,' he said mildly.

'Because if I stayed in the apartment all the time,' she said angrily, 'I'd go crazy. Rory persuaded me to go somewhere quiet to eat something, which I couldn't do when we got there anyway. He ate my helping too. That man took the photograph while Rory was trying to make me believe that it was all going to end happily. You said you'd spoken to the Press.'

'I asked them for their co-operation,' he said. 'I wanted this whole affair kept low-key. Nearly all of them have gone along scrupulously with my wishes but I can't muzzle those who won't.'

'I see.' She bit her lip, anger diminishing into hopelessness.

'Are you sure you're not over-reacting because you're not sitting at home wringing your hands?' he asked. 'If that's in your mind rest assured you're mistaken. You have to lead as normal a life as possible until this is cleared up.'

'And when will that be?' Anger woke in her again, impotent and burning. 'It's nearly five days since Sally

was taken. Five days! And there's no clue to tell us why
she was taken or where. Yes, I know there might have
been if I'd told you about the second note, but I didn't
and you can't depend on the people who took her
sending little notes to make it easier for you. I want to
know what's being done. The phone-ins aren't working;
the television appeal hasn't brought anything useful.
What do you do next?'

'We go on plodding away until we get a break,' he
said.

'Yes, of course.' She looked at him wearily. 'That's the
standard reply. You never close a case when it involves
the disappearance of a child. Even if she never comes
back every time another child is stolen you take down
the files and mull over the details of this case all over
again.'

'I trust we can do better than that for you, Miss
Prentice.' His look was not without sympathy. 'We'll go
on investigating every possible lead and sooner or
later –'

'You'll get a break, I heard it before.'

'I work on facts, Miss Prentice, not hunches,' he said,
'but every police officer gets the occasional hunch.
They're not infallible, but they often work out. I have
the feeling that this whole affair has a dimension we
haven't yet fathomed. When we work that one out then
we'll be nearer getting Sally back.'

'Thank you anyway.' Subdued, she rose, watching
him crumple up the newspaper and aim it accurately
into a waste paper basket in the corner. Before she had
left the office his head was bent over a file again.

Rory would be with her in the afternoon. The
prospect of that was more than a comfort. She had
begun to depend on the certainty of seeing him. Five
days was too short a time to be sure of her own feelings,
she warned herself, but the warmth about her heart

when she thought of Rory remained. Perhaps in a crisis one's emotions were intensified, speeded to maturity under stress. And when the stress was lifted and she had Sally home again – please God let Sally come home!

It was a disappointment when she reached the apartment block to see Hal climbing out of his car. 'I thought I told you to leave,' she said coldly as he strode up to her.

'I saw the newspaper this morning,' he said. 'I wanted you to know that I didn't have anything to do with that photograph.'

'I didn't think you had, but thanks anyway.' She made to go past him but he caught at her arm, his face pleading. 'I stayed around because I hoped – Joy, you're still a lovely woman. I guess I made a big mistake when I walked out on you.'

'Some mistakes can't be rectified. Leave me alone, Hal.'

'You're not as indifferent as you pretend,' he said, still holding her arm. 'you couldn't be. When I saw you again I felt all the old emotions come sweeping back.'

'Then I'm sorry.' She tugged her arm free. 'I got over you a long time ago, Hal. I'm truly sorry if you're starting to think that you made a mistake, but there isn't anything I want to do about it.'

'You still hate me,' he said sadly.

'No, I don't,' she said truthfully. 'I don't feel anything for you at all. You're just not important in my life any more. It really is all over.'

'It's that Canadian fellow, isn't it?' His brilliantly blue eyes had narrowed. 'Rory Baird? Maybe you ought to check him out a bit more carefully before you rush into anything.'

'Goodbye, Hal.'

She cut him short icily and went inside, mounting the stairs without looking back, feeling a coldness at the core of herself because it really was over.

Rory would be here soon to set her doubts at rest –

what doubts? She was falling in love with Rory, wasn't she, so what doubts could there be? Hal had spoken out of wounded pride and jealousy because his self image was damaged by the thought that she could prefer any other man to himself. He wasn't really interested in having her back. He merely wished to make certain that emotionally she was still bound to him. Rory Baird, history teacher from Toronto, meeting her by chance in the little cemetery. The police had surely checked him out. She was safe in trusting him.

She unlocked her door, entering the silent living room, closing the door behind her, fighting a sudden uncertainty that was gnawing at her. Some words could be dangerous things, dripping poison into clear water.

'Hot strong coffee,' she said aloud. She mustn't allow herself to go to pieces now. Five days were not so long. Her mind shuddered away from the prospect of all the days ahead. When her doorbell rang she almost spilled the coffee. Surely to God Hal wasn't about to invite another rebuff. It was more likely to be Rory. Opening the door she looked down at the little boy who stood there. A neighbour's son. She knew him by sight but not by name.

'Yes?' She forced a polite, questioning smile.

'A man gave me this for you,' the boy said. He was holding out a letter.

It was utterly stupid but the first thought that came into her mind was that Rory had thought things over and decided to cut loose and fly home. With the thought came the realisation that her own insecurity must be very deep. She would have to remember that before she flung herself into any new relationship.

'What man where?' She spoke so sharply that the boy took a step back.

'On the way from school,' he said defensively. 'The man gives me the letter and says it's for Miss Prentice. That's you.'

'What did the man look like?' Taking the envelope she calmed her voice with an effort.

'He was in a car,' the boy said. 'Had a peaked cap on. I never saw his face proper.'

'A big black car?' As he nodded she asked urgently. 'Did you get the number?'

'I only collect train numbers,' he said.

'And you didn't see his face?'

'No. I was running home,' the boy said. 'It's dinner time.'

'Yes, well – thank you very much.'

Closing the door as he scooted down the stairs again, presumably to eat his dinner, she stood, holding the letter. There were more questions to ask the boy but the police would do that. This time she was going to be sensible and tell them. Her fingers twitched nervously as she opened the thick, creamy envelope and drew out the single piece of paper it contained. 'SHOCKED BY NEWSPAPER ITEM. HOPE YOU ARE FIT MOTHER FOR SALLY.' And that was all.

Seven

'This could be the breakthrough we've been waiting for.' Detective Fuller said. His voice was ironed flat of anything that might conceivably be interpreted as excitement. Rory had arrived as she was reading the message and driven her straight to the police station. Detective Fuller had met them in the reception area, on his way to snatch a bite at the local pub, as he informed them. Instead he had sent out for coffee and sandwiches, though Joy had no idea whether she had eaten ham or cheese. Ken and Mavis were there too, both looking professionally bright and alert.

'Fingerprints?' Rory asked. 'Not a one. I wouldn't expect any. The main point is that Sally appears to be alright.'

'How do you know? A hunch?' Joy leaned forward, her eyes on his face.

'Not only that, Miss Prentice. Not absolute proof either, I'm afraid, but what might be termed internal evidence. The writer says "are a fit mother", not "were". I know it's a small point but it is a point. I'd venture further. The content of the note might be somewhat insulting to Miss Prentice but it betrays a definite concern for the child's welfare.'

'You're not suggesting that Sally was taken away because someone thought that I wasn't looking after her properly?'

'That's highly unlikely. From my own observation I'd say that you did wonders in very difficult circumstances, but every tiny piece of information, no matter how apparently insignificant, helps us build up a composite picture of the man or men.'

'Or woman?' Rory said.

'So far all the signs point to its being a man, or as I'm inclined to believe, men,' Detective Fuller said. 'On the one hand we have an elderly gentleman afflicted by an obsession. He writes three notes, each one betraying some concern for Sally. He has to be reasonably affluent and well educated since he uses good quality notepaper and a fountain pen. He also owns or drives – most likely the former – a large black car. On the other hand we have the driver of the car who is, I reckon, younger and more active. He wears a peaked cap and is agile enough to climb high walls. Wears sneakers.'

'Why do you say that?' Joy interrupted.

'You didn't hear footsteps within the cemetery because there's grass and not gravel between the wall and the bench, but anyone getting over the wall in ordinary shoes would be bound to scrape the stone, so I'm betting on his wearing sneakers. I'm also betting on his being fairly tall but not hefty. He left the teddy bear behind him because in all likelihood he couldn't manage to carry a sleeping child and the duffel bag and the toy and close the door behind him. Oh, and it's fairly obvious he knows the area quite well. He's been following you for some time, Miss Prentice, and he cased out the back premises of the Sunset fairly thoroughly.'

'I've never been aware of being followed,' she said helplessly.

'From which I deduce he only tailed you in crowds or that he stayed in the car. You took the bus to the supermarket the other day.'

'You mean he followed the bus?'

'Watched you go into the supermarket and then gave the note to the lad who stacks the baskets. That also tells us that he's an opportunist, delivering the notes as and when the chance comes.'

'He couldn't have known when I was going to leave the teddy bear.'

'He most likely watched you leave the house and go to the cinema. You weren't carrying anything then, so he hung around until later. Parked in the side road and waited for you to walk through the cemetery gates. Then shinned over the wall and took off again.'

'I was afraid to look round too much,' Joy said. 'And it was dark.'

'Do you think we ought to put a tail on Miss Prentice, sir?' Ken asked.

'I rejected that idea at the beginning,' Detective Fuller said. 'I felt it would be wiser to give our quarry a clear field. Now I'm wondering.'

He tapped his teeth thoughtfully with the end of a pencil.

'I couldn't bear knowing that I was being followed round all the time,' Joy said.

'But you've been followed for quite a time already if our deductions are correct,' he said.

'I wasn't aware of it,' Joy said. 'Now the whole idea makes me cringe.'

'And it probably wouldn't serve any useful purpose,' Detective Fuller said. 'Not to mention the irritating but undeniable fact that we really can't spare the men for constant surveillance. I'll have a squad car cruise in that area where you live, but it's likely our quarry will keep away from there in future.'

When he said 'quarry' she saw in her mind something hunted, furtive, panting. 'Are you going back to work, Miss Prentice?' he was continuing. She shook her head. 'Ken, you go along and have a word with the lad who gave Miss Prentice this latest note.'

'Sir.' Ken stuffed his notebook in his pocket and stood up.

'Do you know the lad's name?' Detective Fuller looked at Joy.

'Something Taylor, I think. They live on the third floor.'

'He'll be due home from school again shortly. Find out exactly what happened. Give him a ride in the Panda by way of inducement. Go with him, Mavis.'

'Sir,' said Mavis.

They moved out in unison like twins. 'Sensible of you to bring the note to us, Miss Prentice,' Detective Fuller said with faintly reluctant approval. 'Helps us to round out the picture.'

'There's something else we know about the man,' Rory said.

'What's that, Mr Baird?'

'He seems to have a compulsion for writing notes.'

'That's an excellent point.' Rory received a look of unqualified approval. 'He wasn't obliged to write this third note. But he did. He wants to keep us in the picture, so to speak. He's obsessive and compulsive. He'll write again. Now that he's started he'll carry on. Possibly a bid for attention, and a need to prove himself superior to the police. A lonely man.'

'You sound as if you're sorry for him!' Joy burst out.

'Anyone who takes a child for whatever reason will get no compassion from me,' he said, 'but in an unofficial capacity I feel a certain sympathy. I don't expect you to feel the same way.'

'I don't,' Joy said flatly.

'While you're busy building up psychological profiles my little girl is still missing.'

'We're checking every statement, every scrap of information,' he said patiently. 'We've set up an information room and it's buzzing. Sooner or – yes?' He broke off as a policewoman entered.

'Information just came in, sir.' She handed him a typewritten sheet. 'We thought you'd want to see it immediately.'

He was rapidly scanning the typescript. When he looked up his face was less weary. 'This looks like something,' he said, 'though I don't want to raise your hopes. A child with fair hair answering to the name of Sally has just been picked up wandering about down in the dock area. You'd better come with us, Miss Prentice.'

'I can drive Joy,' Rory said.

'Follow the squad car then,' Detective Fuller went out with the policewoman.

'Rory, do you think –?' Instinctively she reached for his

hand.

'Honey, for all our sakes, I'm praying it is,' he said gently. Prayers were not always answered. She had prayed over and over that there had been some terrible mistake and that her parents would come home. It hadn't happened. She pushed the memory away from her and went out to the car.

At mid afternoon the traffic was thinner than it would be later on during the rush hour when people were coming back from work, but the traffic lights all seemed to turn red as they approached and once they lost the police car and inadvertently took a wrong turn out of which Rory had hastily to reverse. Joy sat silently at his side, her nails digging into her palms. Her stomach was churning with fear and anticipation. If it was Sally – it had to be Sally. She couldn't think beyond the moment when she would see her again.

The police station was in a side street. Rory drew up behind the police car and Joy was out on the pavement almost before he had switched off the ignition.

'I hope it's good news,' Detective Fuller said as he went up the steps.

'Detective Fuller?' A thick-set man had emerged from an inner office and was shaking hands. 'You phoned in a report of a child. Miss Prentice. Mr Baird.'

'Miss Prentice. Inspector Leigh.' He shook her hand briskly. 'I'm hoping we have your little girl. The description fits and she insists her name is Sally.'

'If I could see her –?' Despite her resolve her voice shook with excitement.

'In here. Policewoman Collins has charge of –'

Of a small girl with curly fair hair who sat on the edge of the table, her feet swinging. A grubby little girl with a pretty face. Not Sally. Not her Sally. She shook her head mutely and sat down on the nearest chair, fighting for control as the surge of bitter disappointment threatened to overwhelm her.

'She is remarkably like the photograph,' Detective Fuller said.

'We were almost sure,' Inspector Leigh said in an aggrieved tone.

'Couldn't you have made certain before you dragged Miss Prentice down here?' Rory said.

'As she was on the spot when the report came in –' Detective Fuller spread his hands.

'It isn't Sally,' Joy said thickly. 'Not my Sally.'

'There haven't been any reports of any other child missing,' Inspector Leigh began.

'Why don't you suggest that I take this one and save you all the trouble of looking for my Sally?' Joy demanded. 'Or do you think I wouldn't know my own child?'

Rory put his hand on her shoulder and she bit her lip, welcoming the purely physical pain. A woman clutching a shopping basket was hurrying up the steps into the outer offices, starting her sentence before she had even reached the door.

'My little girl's gone missing – in the fish market. I turned round for one minute and when I turned back – looked everywhere. She never did such a thing before!'

A dumpy young woman with her head tied up in a turban. The most fortunate woman in the world. Joy rose wordlessly and went down to the car again.

'I wish I could express –' Detective Fuller was at her side, for once stirred out of his wooden calm. Behind him the constable who had driven him looked all embarrassed sympathy.

'It wasn't your fault,' she heard herself say. 'We all thought it must be Sally.'

'We'll continue investigations,' he said, and she nodded and got into the passenger seat, mechanically fastening the seat belt. Rory, sliding behind the wheel and starting the engine, said doggedly,

'If they can find one child they can find two. If you want to howl and cry now's the time to let it out. I'll be too busy driving to notice.'

'That won't bring her back.' She rubbed her eyelids fiercely with her balled fists. 'It'd relieve my feelings for the moment and give me a headache and Sally would still be lost. I can't spend the rest of my life weeping. It won't help.'

'You set high standards for yourself.' He slanted her a quick, warm smile.

'Then I'll have to live up to them, won't I?' she retorted. 'Rory, this isn't your problem. Whatever might be growing between us it still isn't your problem. You have the right to walk away.'

'I'm not availing myself of it.' He sent her another brief smile. 'Where do you want to go?'

'The apartment, please.' She sat up straighter. 'I want to tidy out Sally's drawers. I want to have all her things clean and neat for when she comes home.'

'No company?'

'No company. I need to be by myself, getting ready for Sally's return.'

'Did I ever tell you, Joy Prentice, that you're quite a lady?' he said. She smiled, feeling the sobs thicken in her throat, holding them back. 'I think that I'll get my own researches into my ancestors into some kind of order,' Rory was saying.

'Did you find out anything more?' She bestirred herself to answer.

'My attention's been on other matters,' he said dryly, 'but I think I've got sufficient information to please my parents when I get back. It was Great-great-aunt Eulalia's brother who emigrated to Canada. I was hoping I might stumble across another branch of the family but it seems not. Will I see you tomorrow? You said you decided not go back to work.'

'It was more or less decided for me. After that news-paper item Mrs Clark feared that I might drag down the high reputation of the Sunset.'

'Then sue for wrongful dismissal,' he said.

'I couldn't be bothered,' she told him. 'You can't alter unreasonable prejudice.'

'I guess you're right. Are you sure you can manage for —?'

'Quite sure,' she cut in. 'Oh, Hal came by.'

'Again? What did he want?'

The jealousy in his voice made her almost light hearted. She had almost forgotten how it felt to flirt teasingly with a man. 'Me,' she said demurely. 'I told him no deal and he finally realised that I meant what I said. I don't hate him, you know. Sally is physically part of him so I can't hate him, but what I do feel is complete indifference.'

'You can't guess how good that makes me feel.' He took one hand from the wheel and laid it gently against the side of her face as they reached the apartment house.

'Will I see you tomorrow?' She looked at him.

'Tomorrow and every day, I hope. Look, I persuaded you to go to that damned wine bar, so in a way I feel responsible for what happened —'

'You're responsible for helping me to hold myself together,' she said.

'Tomorrow then.'

'If anything comes up before tomorrow give me a ring. Wait, have you any paper?'

'In my bag.'

She tore a page out of her small diary. 'And I've a pen somewhere. Here we are.'

He scribbled on the paper. 'Hotel, room number, telephone number. Is your line still hooked up to the police station?'

'As far as I know.'

'In that case ask them to ring me. Don't go wandering about after dark by yourself.' He had forgotten that she was used to coming home after midnight. She didn't remind him, his care and concern touching her. It was good to feel protected.

'Tomorrow then, if not before.' He kissed her lightly, a kiss that demanded nothing, and leaned to open the car door.

On her way up the stairs a door opened on the landing beneath her apartment and her name was spoken tentatively.

'Miss Prentice?' A woman, thirty-fiveish, pretty in a faded way, was framed in the aperture.

'Mrs Taylor?' Joy paused.

'My boy's been helping the police in their enquiries today,' the woman said proudly. 'Would you like to come in for a cup of tea? At a time like this – well, people ought to be more neighbourly, I think.'

She was probably moved more by curiosity than anything else, Joy thought wearily, but the varied emotions of the afternoon had drained her.

'Thank you.' She went into the apartment, a larger one than her own, as the other moved aside. The room looked cheerfully tasteless with a flight of ducks above the mantelpiece and a large television set dominating the surroundings.

'Do sit down. I have just brewed up,' Mrs Taylor said. 'You know I did want to pop up and see if there was anything I could do, but people get – you know – a bit awkward like at offering help at these times. No word, I suppose?'

'Nothing yet.' Joy shook her head, accepting the cup of tea.

'I hope there wasn't anything bad – upsetting like in the note?'

There was definite curiosity in the woman's voice but Joy felt too tired to be indignant. 'Nothing,' she said. 'It was very helpful of your son to pass it on to me though.'

'Lance is a good boy. He's ever so sorry that he never got the number of the car. Trains is his hobby. That and the telly. If he'd realised –'

'It wasn't his fault. He hardly saw the driver.'

'Youngish with a peaked cap,' Mrs Taylor said.

'And a tattoo,' Lance said, looking up from the comic he was reading.

'What? You never said nothing about a tattoo before!' his mother exclaimed.

'Forgot about it, didn't I? Only just remembered it now.'

'Why now?' Joy asked.

'I collect posters,' he told her. 'Got more than a hundred.'

'Miss Prentice doesn't want to hear about your old posters now.'

'Mrs Taylor, please – go on, Lance.' Joy put down her half finished cup of tea.

'I've got a lot of pop posters and the Star Trek ones and Star Wars – there's a new Star Wars one in my comic this week. I've only just got it.'

'What did it make you remember, Lance?' She spoke softly, not wanting to frighten him off.

His mother was less restrained. 'If you saw something you ought to have told that nice policeman,' she scolded. 'And him giving you a ride in his Panda car too.'

'I forgot,' the boy protested. 'The policeman kept asking me if I remembered anything about the man's face and I kept trying to think. He had gloves on and he give me the letter through the car window. Then right now, as I was looking at my comic and this week's poster, I remembered he had a tattoo on his wrist. His coat sleeve went up a bit when he was giving me the letter, see, but I didn't think no more about it at the time.'

In a moment she would scream. Joy took a deep breath and said, 'What sort of tattoo, Lance?'

'A circle,' Lance said. 'A circle with letters inside it. DV. Darth Vader from Star Wars, like this week's poster, see? That's what made me remember it.'

'You're sure now?' his mother demanded. 'You're not just making this up to get another ride in the Panda car?'

'Honest, mum!' he said in an injured tone. 'DV for Darth Vader. The bottom half of the circle was hidden by his glove but I saw the letters plain as plain. DV.'

'Is it important, d'ye think?' Mrs Taylor asked anxiously. 'Ought we to go down to the station? I've got my husband's tea to get.'

'I'll pass on the information,' Joy said. 'They might want to see Lance again.'

'I'm helping the police in their enquiries,' Lance said.

'Will he be here if they come round now?' Joy rose to go.

'Oh, we don't let him go running about after dark,' said Mrs Taylor. 'You never know what might happen these days with all these maniacs –'

She broke off, reddening to the roots of her faded fair hair.

'I'll telephone the station immediately,' Joy said, taking pity on her. 'Thank you for the tea. Maybe I'll see you again very soon.'

Going out she ran up the remaining flight of stairs and let herself into her own apartment. First the telephone call. They hadn't said anything about disconnecting the line. Dialling, she wondered if Detective Fuller had gone home – if indeed he ever did manage to go home. His flat, nasal voice answered however. 'Detective Fuller here.'

'Joy Prentice.' She tried to match the crispness of his tone. 'The boy, Lance Taylor, who gave me the last note just remembered something else.'

'Yes?' His voice had sharpened.

'The man who gave him the note had a tattoo on his wrist. The boy only just remembered it.'

'What sort of tattoo?'

'A circle with the letters DV inside it. Does that mean anything?'

'Indeed it does.' There was satisfaction in the voice now. 'Look, I'll come straight over. Is the boy still at home?'

'Yes.'

'Be there in ten minutes.' He hung up abruptly. There wasn't time for a bath. She took a quick shower and twisted her hair into a knot. By the time she had slipped into skirt and sweater the expected ring came at the doorbell. Ken was with Detective Fuller, both men looking like bloodhounds who have scented the fugitive.

'We're going down to have a word with the boy,' the latter said. 'Would you like to come with us?'

'Yes, I would.' Joy said promptly.

'Your presence seems to have a good effect on his memory,' Detective Fuller said.

When they reached the lower floor Mrs Taylor had already opened her door, and ushered them into a room that had obviously received a hasty tidy-up. The used tea cups had been whisked out of sight: the television set now supported a vase of artificial roses; Lance looked suspiciously damp round the ears.

'Do come in. Excuse the mess.' Mrs Taylor sounded half nervous, half excited.

'Sorry to trouble you again, Mrs Taylor. I'm Detective Fuller. My colleague you already know, I believe.'

'Yes indeed.' She fluttered vaguely in Ken's direction, then hastily motioned them to chairs.

'Nice place you have here, Mrs Taylor,' Detective Fuller said. 'Very cosy.'

'A cup of tea?' she hovered uncertainly.

'I wouldn't say no. A nice cuppa's always welcome, isn't it, Ken?' The detective rubbed his hands together and beamed at Lance.

'I told Miss Prentice what I remembered,' Lance said defensively.

'And very properly too,' Detective Fuller said. 'I wish all our witnesses were as accurate. Now I'd like to hear it from you personally and then we can get everything absolutely straight.'

'He won't get into trouble for not remembering everything right off, will be?' Mrs Taylor asked nervously, coming in with tea. Joy accepted a second cup, trying to recall if she'd drunk her first one.

'No question of trouble,' Detective Fuller said. His heartiness sat uneasily on him. 'How old are you, Lance?'

'Eleven next month,' Mrs Taylor said.

'Is that so, Lance?' Without actually saying anything Detective Fuller managed to convey that he wanted the boy to answer. Mrs Taylor flushed slightly and sat down at the corner of the table with her cup of tea.

'That's right,' Lance said, adding politely, 'Sir.'

'I take it you go to the local comprehensive?'

'Standard One,' Lance said.

'And you were on your way home for dinner when the car drew up. You don't stay for school dinners?'

'I like to know he's had a home-cooked meal,' his mother put in defensively.

'I'm told school meals aren't too bad these days,' Detective Fuller said. 'When I was a boy they were pretty horrible. Now, Lance, the car drew up and the man leaned out and told you to give the letter to Miss Prentice. Did you know Miss Prentice?'

'I see her sometimes,' Lance said, 'but I didn't know as how she was called Miss Prentice. The man in the car told me she lived on the fourth floor. Her name's on the door.'

'And you've remembered the man had a tattoo on his wrist?'

'Like this.' Lance darted to the other end of the table and returned with a brightly tinted poster.

'What colour was it?'

'Blue,' Lance said promptly. 'Very bright blue.'

'You're sure about that?'

'It was covered by his glove and his sleeve but I saw it when he reached out to give me the letter, but I didn't realise then that I saw it,' Lance said painstakingly.

'And then what happened?'

'He drove off fast,' Lance said.

'What sort of car was it?'

'A big black one,' Lance said. 'Posh.'

'Well polished, would you say?'

'Very shiny,' Lance said.

'Anyone in it except the man?' The boy shook his head. 'And can you repeat exactly what the man in the car said?'

'I told the other policeman,' Lance said, nodding towards Ken.

'I'm checking he got it down right. He's apt to be a bit careless,' Detective Fuller said unblushingly.

Lance screwed his eyes shut, took a deep breath and said,

'He said, "Hey, you live there in that building?" I said "yes", but I kept on walking like mum told me to when a stranger talks to me. Then he said, "Can you give this to Miss Prentice? She lives on the fourth floor." Then he gives me the letter and drives off fast.'

'Any special kind of voice?'

'Just ordinary. Like mine but more grown up,' Lance said.

'Looked like a criminal, did he?' Detective Fuller enquired.

'I don't know,' Lance said. 'I never met anyone criminal.'

'Indeed he hasn't.' Mrs Taylor put in vigorously.

'And he was wearing –?' Detective Fuller neatly elbowed her out without actually doing anything.

'Peaked cap, shiny peak,' Lance said.

'Jacket?'

'Dark blue, sort of an overcoat,' the boy said.

'But not a uniform?' Lance shook his head.

'What about the gloves?'

'Brown ones,' Lance said. 'Sort of leather.'

'And now you've remembered about the tattoo?'

'I'd have remembered it before,' Lance said, 'but I got excited about having a ride in the Panda car.'

'Aye, it's a wonderfully exciting life, being a policeman,' Ken said.

'You're sure there's nothing else you've remembered?' Detective Fuller looked straight at Lance.

'No, sir.' Lance looked straight back.

'Seems clear enough.' Detective Fuller nodded. 'We're very grateful to you, Lance. We are indeed. You've been a big help.'

'I got a ride in the Panda car last time,' Lance hinted broadly.

'Tell you what, Mrs Taylor, why don't you bring Lance down to the station a week from tomorrow? Now that'll be a Saturday so if you bring him over at say – ten o'clock, then I'll have the pair of you given a guided tour. But only the once. If you happen to remember anything else you tell us for free.'

'I don't remember anything else,' Lance said honestly.

'Fine.' Detective Fuller rose to his feet. 'You've a fine boy there, Mrs Taylor. Also a delicate hand with the brewing of tea. Wish my missus had. Thank you.'

They returned to Joy's apartment, leaving behind a satisfied and self-important Lance and a highly gratified Mrs Taylor.

'Nice lad,' Detective Fuller said. 'Pity he didn't come

up with this earlier. You should have pressed a mite harder before you knocked everything else out of his head with that ride round.'

'Sorry, sir,' Ken said woodenly.

'What does the tattoo mean?' Joy asked. She had sat, holding down her impatience while the detective had slowly drawn out the information from the boy, but now her voice came out sharply.

'The DV within the circle in bright blue? May I –?' He indicated a chair.

'I'm sorry. Please. The tattoo?'

'There's a Halfway House – you know what that is?'

'No.'

'Fairly young offenders just released from gaol often spend a period in what is called a Halfway House until they find their feet in the community again. Sometimes it works, and sometimes it doesn't. A couple of years back, in one of the Halfway Houses, there was a craze for tattooing. Some of the lads – most of them are young offenders – had the letters DV put in a circle on their wrists, kind of a mark of brotherhood. All rather childish and harmless, but it means that our driver is almost certainly from that particular House. Now we check the records, find out who has skipped or hasn't reported to his Probation Officer recently. They've already got onto that down at the station.'

'But won't there be an awful lot of names to check?' Joy said unhappily.

'True, but the one we're looking for can drive a car, knows the London districts, is agile and speaks without any particular accent. When we find him then we can move in.'

'You don't think it's a gang, do you?'

'Has all the earmarks of one man initiating events and employing someone to carry out the action. Not a gang. I'm going to send a man round to question your neighbours again. Now there are eight apartments here, two on each floor, right?'

'Yes.'

'Someone might have noticed the boy talking to the driver of the car. What's on the top floor?'

'Above here? Attics. Why?'

'Ken?' He nodded towards the policeman who went out at once.

'Why would you want to know –?' She broke off, images of horror rising in her mind.

'In nine cases out of ten crimes against the person are committed either by relatives or neighbours – no, you aren't in my list unless you're the greatest actress the world has ever known, and we have checked out your immediate neighbours, but it won't do any harm to check the attics.'

'You do think she's dead?' Joy whispered. 'You do, don't you?'

'My instincts tell me she isn't but I can't afford to rely entirely on my instincts.'

Ken came in again, brushing dust from his uniform. 'Nothing but old sacks and packing cases – all empty.' he said. 'The floor boards aren't too healthy.'

'I didn't think there would be anything but it never hurts to eliminate,' Detective Fuller said. 'Come on, Ken, I hope you didn't have a date tonight.'

'Not any more,' Ken said wryly, following his superior to the door.

'We'll be in touch.' The other turned to nod at Joy. 'I'm sorry about the fiasco earlier on today.'

'It wasn't your fault,' she said dully. 'I got my hopes up too high, that's all.' By now that other Sally would be tucked up in bed, scolded and cuddled and safe, her mother telling her husband of the fright she'd had, both of them agreeing that it was a terrible world when you couldn't let a small child out of your sight.

If she allowed her mind to continue along that channel she would go crazy. Better to fix her mind on the tattoo which was a sure lead to the driver of the car. 'Don't start getting your hopes up too high again,' she warned herself aloud. She made herself a tomato sandwich and ate it standing up by the window, looking out into the darkness of the street. Beyond the roofs and the wall the tombstones gleamed faintly. It was better not to think of them either.

It was a pity she had told Rory not to come. She wanted to tell him about this new development, to have her rising hopes bolstered by his own calm confidence. She could ask the police to contact him.

The nearest call box was a couple of streets away. She had promised Rory not to go out into the dark alone which was all nonsense because it was little girls who were being snatched away, but a promise was a promise. She could ask one of her neighbours if she could use their telephone. One or two had nodded at her recently, acknowledging her existence, but they hadn't stopped to chat. Nobody wanted the mother of a missing child in too intimate contact. It was almost as if people feared that troubles were infectious. She would call the station. Rummaging in her bag for the hotel number she reflected that this situation was changing her, draining away her powers of decision in quite small matters. If something didn't happen very soon she would be unable to function.

Here it was. His name, room and hotel number. Rory Baird. Unusual handwriting, the slope sharp, the letters elongated, the y double looped. She had seen it before – somewhere. But Rory had never written anything to her. Yet his writing was familiar. She went on staring at it.

Eight

The whole world was suddenly insecure. Joy sat down, her eyes fixed on the bold, slanting hand. Rory Baird had become the main bulwark of her tottering universe. She was beginning to fall in love with him. She had known him less than a week. 'This is stupid,' she said aloud. It wasn't stupid. In nightmares everything made its own ghastly sense. Rory had got into conversation with her in the little cemetery and under the stress of events their relationship had blossomed very quickly – too quickly? He had been with her on and off ever since, involved in every twist and turn of the investigation.

It was like looking down into a clear pool of water and seeing at the bottom a mass of tiny crawling things. Was there a third person involved who could make regular reports to the other two exactly what was going on? But even that didn't explain how it was she knew his handwriting.

She grabbed her own pen and paper and began compulsively to make notes, anything to make herself feel as if she were doing something. 'Elderly man. Compulsive. Obsessive. Non-driver? Invalid? Young man. Tattooed, criminal record, drives car, knows area, probably followed me and Sally. Hal. Cheap extortion stunt? Not likely.

'Rory Baird.' She stared at the last name, then wrote rapidly. 'Schoolteacher from Toronto, over here to look up his ancestors. Police will have checked that. Said he wasn't going to pick me up but in actual fact did pick me up. Hired a car and came to collect me from the Sunset.

Has been around ever since. Says he wants a deeper relationship. Took me to the wine bar where the newspaper photograph was taken.'

Nothing made any sense. There was no reason for anyone to go to such lengths to take Sally. There was no ransom involved, no disgruntled husband wanting custody. She crumpled up the paper in exasperation and put it into the small rubbish bin under the sink. She wouldn't ring Rory now but would try to get some sleep instead. In the morning things might be clearer.

She was too emotionally tired to fall asleep at once but lay willing herself not to toss and turn until she dozed off into a troubled dream where she moved through a thick fog towards someone she couldn't see.

She had gone to bed too early and consequently woke up shortly after five. A fine white mist lay over the street, reminding her of her dream. Her brain felt sluggish as if too many questions were weighing it down.

She drank two cups of black coffee while she waited for the water to heat, then took a long bath willing the stiffness out of her limbs, washing her hair until it was squeaky clean. Doing as many practical things as usual postponed the moment when she would have to face her doubts and fears again.

She was finishing off a third cup of coffee and forcing down a slice of toast when the bell announced Rory.

'You look better,' he greeted her, kissing her on the cheek as she resumed her seat. 'May I help myself to a cup of coffee? I've spent most of the night sorting out dead and buried Bairds.'

'I'm afraid my problems have held you up.'

'Don't be silly. They're a lot more important. Any more news?'

'Lance Taylor remembered that the driver of the car had a tattoo on his wrist, a circle with the letters DV inside it. Detective Fuller says that some young men with criminal records staying at a Halfway House had a craze for tattooing a couple of years back, so that's being checked out.'

'Then there is a criminal element involved! Sorry.' He grinned at her over the rim of the coffee cup. 'That was an idiotic thing to say. This whole affair is criminal. What I mean is that this isn't a case of two upstanding citizens suddenly kidnapping a child. This man with the tattoo was obviously hired to carry out the job. That brings up another point.'

'What?'

'The man behind this must have money. I imagine it isn't cheap to hire someone to carry out a kidnapping. He drives a big car too – or rather his associate does.'

'The man with the tattoo.' Joy shivered suddenly. Until now the people who had taken Sally had been faceless and anonymous. Now she could picture the wrist between the edges of sleeve and glove with the initialled circle. DV. Darth Vader.

'Hey there.' Rory leaned forward, tilting up her chin. 'Don't go imagining horrors now when things are starting to look up. They'll find the tattooed man and he'll tell them where Sally is.'

'Last evening the police went up into the attics here, to look for –' Her voice died into a dry and painful sob.

'And found nothing obviously,' Rory said. 'The point is that their minds are working more and more along those lines,' Joy said.

'They have to think of every possibility,' he reassured her.

'I suppose so.' She drew a quivering breath and sipped her coffee.

'Hey!' Rory spoke gently. 'Don't go to pieces now. It may all be over bar the shouting.'

'If they find the tattooed man what guarantee is there that he'll tell the police where Sally is?'

'There aren't any surefire guarantees about anything, but my hunches are usually right,' he said.

'Are they?' Looking at his pleasant face with its blunt features and steady blue eyes she was swept by doubt. Perhaps she'd been a fool to let him know about the tattoo. There had been a time when she had believed Hal to be utterly sincere.

'I'm just stretched too tightly,' she said. 'You know when I first discovered that Sally was missing I didn't know how I was going to get through the next few hours until they brought her back and now I'm beginning to wonder how I'll get through the next few weeks.'

'One day at a time,' he said. 'There'll be more information soon.'

'I'm even beginning to dread that,' she said with a shiver. 'What if the news is bad news? What if Sally's dead? At least now I've got the hope of having her back —'

'It's Saturday today,' he interrupted. 'What would you like to do?'

'Nothing, anything. I'd like to call in at the station and find out if there've been any developments.'

'Wouldn't Detective Fuller have contacted you if there had been?' He glanced at the telephone.

'I suppose so. I feel as if I'm holding them up when I keep asking for news. I want to stay within call anyway. You don't have to stay and hold my hand, you know. I'm a big girl now.'

'We'll have another cup of coffee and decide. No rush.'

He rose to pick up the two cups. It felt right for him to be here, she thought in confusion. Why couldn't she come out with the question that nagged at her then? 'Funny, but I could swear I knew your handwriting already.' She couldn't say it. She couldn't say anything. Rory was too sensitive to her moods. He put down the cups and looked at her.

'What's wrong, Joy?' he asked quietly. 'What's wrong?'

She began to pleat the edge of her skirt. 'Well, Sally's gone – isn't that sufficient for heaven's sake?'

'I don't mean Sally. I mean us. Something's happened and I can't put my finger on what it is. I only know that something's changed between us.'

'When we met –', she began hesitantly.

'I said I wasn't trying to pick you up. That wasn't entirely true. I saw you come along with the little girl and the job of sorting out my ancestors became rather less absorbing than it had been a minute or two before. I did want some excuse to strike up a conversation.'

'Was that the first time you'd seen me – in the cemetery?'

'Yes, of course. You think I followed you there? Joy, what bee have you got in your bonnet now?' He was staring at her.

'The note you gave me yesterday with your name and hotel –'

'In case you wanted to ring.'

'I recognised the handwriting,' she said. 'It's a distinctive hand and I've seen it before.' She stopped abruptly, seeing colour flood his face, the evidence of guilt in his expression. In that instant she wanted to call back her illusions, even if they were wrong. She had once believed that Hal was different from what he had proved to be. She couldn't go through it a second time.

'Caught!' he said unexpectedly, the guilt melting into rueful amusement.

'I don't understand.'

'I ought to have realised – wait.' He stepped over to the small flat-topped desk where she kept her typewriter. 'This is why you recognised my hand. It slipped my mind that you might.' He was holding up the manuscript she hadn't yet begun to type.

'The Case Of The Paper Doll,' Joy said blankly.

'I brought it with me meaning to type it myself while I

was here, but it seemed stupid to spend my time on it when there was so much to see and do, so I gave it to a Typing Agency.'

'You're John Lime,' she said.

'Unpublished writer of mystery novels,' he said ruefully. 'No, that's not quite accurate. I have had a couple of short serials taken over in Canada, but this was my first full-length effort. I was hoping to submit it to a British publisher while I was here so I dropped it in at a local Agency.'

'But why didn't you tell me?'

'Sooner or later I would have done,' he said, looking embarrassed. 'Our relationship has evolved so rapidly and in such an unusual way – and I didn't know that you were the one who was typing it. When I saw my manuscript on the desk I was astonished at the coincidence. When you think about it I suppose it isn't so strange, because the Agency is in the area, and you did mention that you took in typing work.'

'You noticed it the first night?'

'When I stayed over. I saw it on the desk. I meant to tell you about it in the morning but it didn't seem the appropriate time to go chattering on about my own ambitions, perhaps making you feel bad because you weren't settling down to type it. And I was afraid you might imagine that I'd followed you to nag you about the book, so I let it ride.'

'You're John Lime.' She shook her head slowly, relief coursing through her.

'John is my father's name and the Lime – shades of Harry Lime and the Third Man, I suppose.'

'I hadn't even begun to type it,' she said. 'I glanced over it before I took Sally to the cemetery and I suppose the handwriting stayed in my mind. And then I began to think –'

'That somehow or other I might be connected with Sally's disappearance?'

'I realise that it was stupid. The truth is that I'm so worried and confused that I don't know what to think any longer. I simply don't know.' She swallowed painfully, blinking back tears.

'In the beginning I spoke to you partly because you attracted me and partly because it did strike me as a lonely spot for you and the little girl to be in,' Rory said. 'I didn't know you were the one who was typing my novel and after I found out there was never a right time to mention it. Look, I don't want you to feel that I've moved into your life without giving you any options. You can check up on me, if you like, but I really do care about you and Sally and I am exactly what I claim to be.'

'I feel a complete fool,' Joy said.

'It was bright of you to recognise the handwriting.' He bent to touch her cheek with the back of his hand. 'Now what are we going to do today?'

Before she could answer the doorbell rang, heralding Detective Fuller who entered with his usual air of weariness.

'We've made some progress,' he said with only the briefest of greetings. 'There are three men who fit the bill. No coffee, thanks.'

'The man with the tattoo?' Joy asked urgently.

'One of the fellows we were interested in is back inside. The other's still at the Halfway House but he seems clean, has held down a responsible job for the past year and is planning to get married. He's still a possibility but an increasingly unlikely one. The third man sounds more promising from our point of view. The third man's done a bunk, about six months ago. He left the Halfway House and hasn't reported to his Probation Officer.'

'Who is he?' she asked tensely.

'Name of Jimmy Hargreaves. Age twenty-two. Petty thief, no record of violence or assault. He can drive, knows the area well and is slightly built but fairly athletic. Apparently it was a disappointment when he walked out. They told me he'd been there a couple of years and gave every sign of going straight. Anyway there's an all-points alert out for him.'

'He just left? He didn't mention where he was going?' Rory asked the question.

'Where is the Halfway House?' Joy cut in.

'Ebury Place, but there's no sense in your going round there. Believe me, but we've made all the relevant enquiries. He left without a word, but we've every hope of picking him up soon. So, I'll be in touch.'

'I appreciate it, your coming here,' Joy said.

'I'm on my way home for a couple of hours,' he told her, 'before the wife divorces me.'

He sketched a salute and went, presumably to mend his marriage.

'I think that I can guess where you want to go today,' Rory said as she turned from the door.

'Is it stupid of me?' she asked anxiously. 'I know the police have been there already but I'm Sally's mother. Someone might say something to me when they wouldn't talk to the police.'

'We've nothing to lose. Come on.' Not one word of disappointment because she hadn't trusted him, Joy thought. She met his eyes and he paused, putting his arm about her shoulders. 'Thanks for not being furious that I didn't confide in you about the novel before,' he said.

'Thanks for not being furious that I haven't got around to typing it yet,' she said. Consulting the street map in the hired car she wondered if the detective had banked on her doing exactly what she was doing.

'It's a fair drive yet. Better lean back and relax,' Rory said, glancing at her without much hope. Her pale face and shadowed eyes had a haunted quality.

'I'll be navigator. The Saturday morning traffic is no joke,' she said firmly.

He was a skilful driver, handling the car with ease. Watching his hands on the wheel Joy had a sudden vision of them caressing her flesh and felt a sense of shock. Her only child was still missing and old sexual desires were stirring. Or was it truly the beginning of love and if it was how much of it was called forth by her own grief and need?

The streets were crowded with people, and most of them seemed to have their children with them. Once as he slowed to round a curve she saw Sally and opened her mouth to cry out. Then the child turned her head and became another child, like Sally only in having fair hair. Joy closed her mouth tightly and felt the seat belt like a steel band around her heart.

'This looks like it.' Rory had turned the car into a wide square, once clearly a district where wealthy manufacturing families had lived, now sunk to shabbiness. The building with its discreet sign Halfway House was on the left and seemed originally to have been two adjoining houses.

'Look at that fanlight,' Rory said as they got out of the car. 'Georgian, if I'm not wrong. Tucked away at the back of nowhere. England's full of surprises.'

'Yes.' Joy's answer was vague. At that moment she had scant interest in historical antiques. The interior was as shabby as the outside though the yellowed mouldings of the high ceiling hinted at past glories. There was a splendidly curving staircase that quarrelled violently with the cheap linoleum on the wooden floors.

A woman on her way down the curving staircase quickened her pace as she saw them standing in the hall below and reached them in something of a rush, her flowered smock ballooning about her ample frame. In contrast to her buxom figure her face was a narrow white wedge, surrounded by a mass of unexpectedly rich red hair. All her vitality seemed concentrated in that, even her voice being flat and colourless. 'Good morning. May I help you?'

'This is Miss Prentice, the mother of the little girl who's missing,' Rory began.

'Ah, yes, I saw you on the television.' The woman shook hands, the frown on her brow intensifying. 'The police were here. We did help them as much as possible. I'm Ruth Jones, one of the team here.'

'Team?' Joy queried.

'The people who come to us are on their way back into a normal life,' Ruth Jones said, 'but one cannot just pluck a criminal – even a petty criminal – from prison and expect him to reintegrate without some counselling, some tactful supervision. We're a small team, but a dedicated one.'

'And you know Jimmy Hargreaves?' Rory asked.

'Oh yes indeed. We counted him as one of our successes so it was quite a disappointment when he left.'

'He ran away?'

'Not ran off, not to say precisely that. He was free to leave as it happens. Most of our people are with us for months rather than years and weeks rather than months. One does encourage them to stand on their own feet as quickly as possible. However as Jimmy had no family he stayed on longer than most. He was on three years probation, you see. When his probationary period was up he still used to go along and visit with Mr Bates. Emotional dependence, you see.'

'Do they work while they're here?' Joy asked. She was not much interested in Jimmy Hargreaves' emotional dependence.

'Either work or train or something. Please come in.' She was leading the way into an office that had once been a handsome drawing room. 'We do recommend that they tell their prospective employers about their pasts and most of them do so, but it's not obligatory. Jimmy wasn't a hardened old lag, not by any means – rather light fingered and a bit wild – deprived home background. It's nearly always the case, isn't it?'

'I wouldn't know,' Rory said shortly. 'You have no idea where he's gone?'

'As I told the police I can't hazard a guess. He was working at a garage when he left. Mechanic. He was always very good with cars. Not many friends. The only one he did get close to unfortunately let himself down.'

'I beg your pardon?' Joy looked at her.

'Went back inside.' Ruth Jones lowered her voice slightly.

'Did Jimmy Hargreaves visit him?'

'Oh no, not at all. They were never close friends.'

'But he was one of those with the tattoo.'

'A very foolish craze. Jimmy went along with the others.'

'That would be two years ago?'

'He hadn't been here long – not fully assimilated. He settled down very well after that.'

'And then he vanished?' Rory pressed.

'Packed his case and went off "for the weekend" he said. 'We do leave them absolutely free to give them a sense of respect. When he didn't turn up after the weekend we did make enquiries at the garage where he was working but he'd given in his notice and left.'

'For no reason?' Rory pressed harder now.

'Said he'd found another job or something. He was entitled to work where he pleased. Part of the rehabilitation programme.'

'Did you have the name of the garage?'

'I had to look it up in the files for the police. Crawfords Garage, near South Street.'

Rory produced the road map, spreading it on the

baize-covered table.

'There.' Ruth Jones stabbed it with a bitten nail.

'Miss Jones.' Joy heard her own voice, very low and strained. 'Would Jimmy Hargreaves be likely to – to harm a small child? You know what I mean. Would he?'

'He has never shown any tendency towards violence,' the other said primly. 'Always very quiet and polite. As I said it was a great disappointment when he left.'

'He wasn't odd in any way?'

She couldn't put her deepest fears into words.

'Only quiet,' Ruth Jones repeated. 'No girl friends. No close friends at all, really. A rather simple young man.'

'Thank you for your help.' Rory folded up the map. 'We'll try the garage.'

'Surely the police will have been there?' Joy objected as they went down the steps.

Behind them Miss Jones speeded them on their way with a plaintive, 'More sinned against than sinning is Jimmy. A most unsatisfactory childhood.'

'You also said that people are sometimes reluctant to say too much to the police. Someone might have remembered something like that lad in your apartment block.'

'I keep thinking there's something that I ought to remember.'

In the car again Joy let herself sag wearily against the upholstered seat.

'Like what?' Rory prompted.

'Something on the edge of my mind,' she told him, 'but every time I try to look at it then it slides out of sight again.'

'It'll come when it's ready. You can't force these things. Our Jimmy doesn't sound like too desperate a character, does he?'

'Weak, influenced by any stronger personality.' Joy sighed. 'That woman was a well intentioned fool.'

'They obviously have some successes or the place

wouldn't still be operational. This garage might yield
more information.'

'He took a job quite a way away,' she commented,
drawing her finger across the section of the map they
were traversing.

'I dare say he wanted to feel independent. Left or
right?'

'Er – left.' She consulted the map again. The feeling
that they were at least trying to do something was better
than sitting and agonising over what might be
happening. It was essential not to think of that.

'Crawford's Garage.'

She opened her eyes as Rory spoke. It was at the end
of a side road, the garage taking up two blocks, the
forecourt littered with vehicles.

'I'll fill her up,' Rory said. 'Why don't you stretch your
legs?'

Joy obeyed, wrinkling her nose at the smell of oil and
gas.

'Can I help you, Miss?' A middle-aged man in stained
overalls hovered near her, studiously avoiding looking
at her legs. 'If you're wanting the Ladies' Room?'

'Oh, no, thank you.' She shook her head smilingly,
adding quickly before he could walk off, 'I wondered if
anyone here was a particular friend of Jimmy
Hargreaves. I'm the mother of the little girl who was
taken.'

'I thought you looked familiar. You were on the telly.'

'Yes, I was. About Jimmy Hargreaves –'

'The police already came.'

'I know, but I wondered if anyone might have
remembered something after they left. I'm so
dreadfully anxious.' Despite her resolve her voice
trembled slightly.

The mechanic's expression became more sympathetic. 'Terrible business,' he said. 'I've two of my own, so I

can guess how you're feeling. Don't think there's anything I can add to what we told the police though. Jimmy left here about six months back. Very quiet lad. Did his own work and minded his own patch so to speak. Left to go to another job. Didn't say where.'

Rory, strolling up to join them, asked, 'Didn't he want a reference?'

'You a policeman?' The suspicion had returned.

'A friend,' Joy said.

'Jimmy said he wanted time out to think things over – wanted to better himself as he put it. The boss said he'd hold the job open for a couple of weeks. He knew Jimmy's record but he decided to give him a chance. Anyway Jimmy took off and that was that. Maybe he went off to stay with his friend.'

'He had a friend?'

'Bit of an exaggeration to call him a friend really. More of a cordial acquaintance.'

'Did you mention this to the police?' Rory asked.

'They wanted to know if he'd any particular friends at the garage which he didn't. Now that you ask me though there was a customer always used to ask for Jimmy to wait on him. Liked the service he gave, I suppose – very quick and polite.'

'Do you know his name? Would it be on his account?'

'No account. He always paid cash. Nice old boy. Funny I forgot all about him until this moment but the police didn't –'

'The customer was old?' Joy willed him to remember.

'Elderly. White moustache. Very clean looking old cove. Posh voice. Jimmy always used to give his car a bit of an extra polish.'

'What type of car?'

'Rover. Dark green. About ten years old but in good condition.'

'Not a large black saloon?' Rory said.

'The police asked about a big black car,' the other said. 'We get plenty of different types of vehicles here in and out – this is a fairly big concern. Can't place any particular one in connection with Jimmy though.'

'And there's nothing else that you can tell us?' Joy asked.

'Sorry, but there isn't anything to tell. Hang on a minute – Patrick!'

He broke off to hail a youngish man who sauntered forward, shifting the cigarette in his mouth from one side to the other.

' 'Morning,' the newcomer said, with a bright inquisitive look.

'This is the lady whose little girl went missing. You recall that old fellow who used to drive in here? Always asked for Jimmy – green Rover? And don't go lighting that fag or you'll get the sack.'

'Sure but the boss can't do without me,' Patrick said in the lilting accent of his native land. 'I was hearing about all the excitement.'

'The police didn't question you?' Rory queried.

'Only just came on shift. Missed all the fun – begging your pardon, Miss. I saw you on the television – makes your blood run cold to think of the murdering villains running round the streets with nobody doing a blind bit to stop them. What about the old fellow?'

'He was Jimmy's friend – acquaintance anyway?'

'Always asked for Jimmy. Haven't laid eyes on him in six months, not since round about the time Jimmy left.'

'Could there be a connection?' Joy clutched at Rory's arm. 'Between the two?'

The other mechanic shrugged.

'Never thought of it. What would you say, Patrick?'

Patrick shifted the unlit cigarette back to the other side of his mouth and mused for a few moments. Then he shook his head. 'Shouldn't think so. Jimmy just used to look after his car – don't think he even mentioned his name. Wait, yes he did. Mr – it's the cars I notice, not the people in them. Mr – Simon. That was it. I recall hearing Jimmy use it one time. "Drive careful, Mr Simon". Polite now you know.'

Nine

'There has to be a connection,' Joy said. 'There simply has to be. It's too much of a coincidence that the man who fits the kidnapper and Sally's invisible friend should have the same name.'

'It was a coincidence my being John Lime,' he pointed out.

'Not such an enormous one,' she countered. 'You were staying in the district and you took your manuscript into the nearest Agency where I happen to collect typing from. But this is the same name.'

'Simon isn't an uncommon name.'

'But we don't know anyone whose name it is. Maybe Sally's Simon isn't as imaginary as I assumed.'

'Sally told you that he's a little boy. Mr Simon is an old fellow with a white moustache.'

'I still think there's a connection.'

'Whether or not the police should be told.' He was heading in the direction of the station. 'It was a piece of luck that Patrick came in when he did.'

'We can't rely on luck, on people suddenly remembering things they forgot to tell the police,' Joy said tightly. 'I've a feeling there's a big piece of – of jigsaw missing and if only that fell into place then Sally would come back.'

'We'll find the piece,' Rory said.

As they got out of the car Detective Fuller alighted from his and turned to assist an elderly woman with fine fluffy white hair. 'Surely not his wife?' Rory said under his breath as the two pairs converged.

'You look as if you have information,' Detective Fuller said. 'Come into the office. This is Miss Carey. Rather convenient meeting up like this.' He didn't explain why it was convenient but went ahead into his office, leaving the other three to follow.

'Please make yourself comfortable. You went round to the Halfway House and then to Crawford's Garage.'

'You're having us followed?' Joy said.

'No, but I reckoned you'd go along there anyway to see if you could find out anything further. It looks as if you have,' Detective Fuller said.

'At the garage.' Joy nodded towards Rory who took up the narrative, speaking briskly and cogently.

'I'll have that followed up,' Detective Fuller said promptly. 'One moment.' He went out leaving them to glance at one another with the tongue-tied politeness of the Anglo-Saxon faced by a complete stranger.

'They ought to have made sure there wasn't anyone on shift duty that hadn't been questioned,' Detective Fuller grumbled, coming in again and sitting down. 'We'll see if we can trace the old gentleman who may have nothing to do with anything of course. What do you think?'

He grappled with a hang nail and looked at Miss Carey.

'Too vague,' the silver-haired lady said.

'Miss Carey occasionally helps us out in certain cases,' he said. 'She has a talent for nosing out valuable information by putting her subconscious mind to work.'

'What he's trying to tell you is that I'm a psychic,' Miss Carey said, looking amused.

'Oh no.' The exclamation broke from Joy. 'I don't believe in any of that mumbo-jumbo.'

'Neither do I,' Miss Carey said surprisingly. 'On the other hand if we were somehow enabled to demonstrate television to a citizen of seventeenth-century London they would regard it as mumbo-jumbo, don't you think?'

'Not when its scientific principles were explained,' Rory said.

'In another century we will probably be able to explain the scientific principles behind such phe- nomena as telepathy and telekinesis,' Miss Carey said. 'My own theory is that it has something to do with electro-magnetic force fields. Do you have anything belonging to Sally? I've seen her photograph and heard the main details of the case, of course.'

Joy hesitated. In the bottom of her bag was a bracelet of blue beads that Sally liked to wear when she was playing parties. The clasp was loose and Joy had meant to have it mended. Reluctantly she handed it over.

'Two children,' Miss Carey said.

'You just heard us mention that Sally has an invisible friend with the same name as the old gentleman who liked Jimmy Hargreaves to service his car,' Joy said.

'This child isn't imaginary,' Miss Carey said definitely. 'A very lively red-haired little boy. Here but not here.'

'I never mentioned the red hair,' Joy said in a low voice to Rory.

'Perhaps she's reading your mind,' he returned.

'That's possible,' Miss Carey said, unoffended. 'One never knows from where the information comes. For some reason the number seventeen keeps coming into my mind. Does that mean anything to either of you?'

'Not to me,' Joy said. 'Rory?'

'Nothing,' he said. 'Well, that's all I'm getting,' Miss Carey said, handing the beads back to Joy. 'Sally is still alive, by the by. Call it a hunch but I feel that very strongly.'

'In which I agree with you,' Rory said.

'I'll have a little meditation later and see if I can come up with anything else,' Miss Carey said, rising. 'Sorry not to have been of more positive help. Good luck.'

'I'll see you out.' Detective Fuller walked her to the door and returned. 'Sometimes we do employ unorthodox means as a channel,' he said, looking defensive. 'Miss Carey is a genuine sensitive. Pity she wasn't able to come up with anything more concrete. Why don't you go home and get some lunch, Miss Prentice? We'll keep you informed.'

'If one more person tells me to go and eat lunch or rest or whatever I think I'll declare war on somebody,' Joy said shakily when they were back in the car.

'What do you want to do?' Rory asked.

Glancing at him Joy said contritely, 'My troubles are ruining your holiday, aren't they?'

'I'm not complaining.' He touched her shoulder lightly. 'The truth is that I've not been sleeping too soundly myself since Sally went. I seem to be developing fatherly feelings.'

'What?' She jerked in her seat.

'Sorry if that was the wrong thing to say. It happens to be true, though.'

'No, it isn't that – you said fatherly feelings.'

'Sounds foolish, I know, since I only met Sally the once. You and I started talking and –'

'And Sally was playing with her ball. She ran off behind the headstones –'

'And?'

They had reached the apartment block and, drawing up, he gave her his full attention.

'She could have talked to someone, couldn't she?' Joy said eagerly. 'Behind the headstones? Some of them are taller than you are.'

'Wouldn't you have seen someone else in the cemetery? Wouldn't I?'

'Not if they were there before we arrived.'

'I'd only been there a couple of minutes before you and Sally came. I don't recall seeing anybody else.'

'Perhaps they were at the other end of the graveyard, behind one of the tombsones or in the shadow of a tree. It is possible, isn't it?'

'I guess so.' He sounded doubtful.

'It was what Sally said later. I've been trying to remember something that seemed very important. After we left you when – no, it was before. Sally ran up and said she'd been talking to Simon's daddy. Rory, you were there. Don't you remember?'

'I remember you were scolding her for going out of sight. She was chattering, but I was too busy looking at you.'

'She said she'd been talking to Simon's daddy,' Joy repeated.

'But if Simon existed his father wouldn't be called Mr Simon,' Rory pointed out.

'Maybe he just told her that to gain her confidence.'

'I don't want to pour cold water on your theory,' Rory said, 'but surely she wasn't gone long enough to strike up a conversation with a complete stranger about her imaginary friend, was she?'

'No, that's true.' Joy heaved a sigh as disappointment rushed in. 'She knew she wasn't supposed to talk to strangers anyway.'

'Perhaps he wasn't a complete stranger,' Rory suggested. 'Perhaps she knew him already?'

'Sally doesn't know anyone I don't know,' Joy said, 'and I know very few people.'

'When you took her to play in the cemetery did you ever talk to anybody? Meet anyone?'

'It's rare for anybody else to be there,' Joy said. 'That's why I go. It's peaceful and safe from traffic.'

'Do you feel like going there now?' he asked abruptly. 'Something else might come into your mind.'

'Let's go there,' she said at once.

The drive took only a couple of minutes. Joy clambered out of the car and went with a quick, swinging stride through the gates. Sunlight dappled the long grass, throwing into relief the lozenge-shaped shadows cast by the tall headstones.

'Do you always sit on the same bench to watch Sally play?' he asked.

'Yes. We come here in the afternoons and the sun shines on that section. Not every afternoon because we go to the park or the playground. I don't actually watch her much. I bring a book and Sally plays up and down. She's very good about not running through the gate.'

'And nobody else ever comes in?'

'The occasional little old lady taking the weight off her feet, the gardener – funny!'

'What's funny?'

'I haven't seen him – the gardener, I mean – for several weeks and in the summer one would think he'd have more work to do. I suppose that officially he's the caretaker.'

'What does he look like?'

'He's just an old fellow who trims the grass sometimes. I don't think I've ever done more than nod to him. Slow, elderly –'

'And?'

'He has a white moustache,' she said slowly.

'And Sally talks to him?'

'I don't know, not for long anyway. I've only seen him a few times. We've exchanged nods. Rory, an old man working part-time in a cemetery wouldn't be driving around in a big car, whether black saloon or green Rover.'

'Do you know if the police have questioned him?'

'I suppose so. I don't know.'

'And he does have a white moustache?'

'Yes, now that I'm thinking about it. Yes, he does. He wears a tweed cap. I never really looked at him properly.'

'I think we'd better nip back to the station and catch Detective Fuller.'

'Let's.' She spoke with energy but the fear that all this was wasted effort crept into her mind.

'Don't start giving up now,' he said as they went back to the car. 'Something's going to come out of all this.' She nodded, drawing comfort from the certainty of his tone.

At the station Detective Fuller was the first person they saw, consulting with the desk sergeant. If he thought they were outwearing their welcome he had the courtesy not to show it, merely greeting them with a nod and the information,

'We've some more sightings to check out though I've not much hope of any of them. Ken had a word with that other mechanic, Patrick Flaherty, but he doesn't recall more than he told you.'

'I wondered if you'd questioned the gardener – cemetery attendant. I'm not sure of his official title,' Joy said.

'What cemetery attendant?' the detective asked.

'The man who cuts the grass at the cemetery.'

'There isn't one.'

'Of course there's one,' Joy contradicted. 'I've seen him working there.'

'That was one of the first things we checked out,' Detective Fuller said without expression. 'We naturally enquired who was employed as caretaker. We were informed that the last attendant retired about a year ago. That whole cemetery is disused now anyway. In time when the area is redeveloped it'll be built over probably. I believe that the local Guiding Association keeps the place in reasonable condition from time to time.'

'How often have you seen this man?' Rory said to Joy.

'Now and then.' She frowned, trying to remember. 'He's a vague figure in the background most of the time, just pottering about.'

'Can you describe him?' Detective Fuller asked.

'Tallish, stooping,' Joy said slowly. 'Wears a tweed cap pulled down to his eyebrows. Has a white moustache, the sort they used to call a walrus moustache. I don't think I ever heard him speak.'

'Then how did you know he was the cemetery attendant?'

'I didn't, I suppose,' Joy said, 'but he acted like one so I assumed he was one.'

'How long have you been taking Sally to the cemetery to play?'

'Since early spring. I used to take her to the playground or the park but then I got the job at the Sunset and sometimes I'm too tired to go very far.'

'There may be a link.'

'There's something else,' she said quickly. 'I've been trying to remember something and then it came to me. Sally told me that she'd been talking to Simon's daddy – her imaginary friend, Simon.'

'The surname of the old gentleman who was friendly with Jimmy Hargreaves,' Rory said.

'The coincidence hadn't escaped me.' Detective Fuller said dryly. 'When did Sally say she'd been talking to Simon's daddy?'

'On the day – the last time I took her to the cemetery

to play. She ran off with her ball while I was talking to Mr Baird and then I called her back.'

'Ran off where?'

'Behind the headstones. It was only for a few minutes. I didn't know anyone else was in the cemetery except Sally and Mr Baird and myself.'

'I didn't see anyone else,' Rory said in answer to the detective's questioning glance. 'I went in to check on my ancestor's headstone and then sat down to make a note on it as Joy and Sally came in.'

'Right then. We'll get on with it,' Detective Fuller said. 'I appreciate all the help you're trying to give. If you recall anything else my office is always open.'

'I wondered if – if Sally's father had gone back north,' Joy said. Odd but she couldn't bring herself to say his name. A name invested someone with a personality and the person she thought she had loved had never really existed.

'Late last night. We checked him out thoroughly, but he's clean – apart from wanting to cash in on the situation. You're better off without him, if you don't mind my saying so,' Detective Fuller said with a bewildering descent into an avuncular manner. 'We'll be in touch with you the minute anything breaks.'

'How about making me some lunch?' Rory suggested when they were in the car again.

'Rory, you must be starving. It's past lunchtime,' she exclaimed.

'Or can I take you somewhere?'

'No, I'll cook something. It will occupy my mind.' She tried to remember what was in the cupboard.

'Anything will do. I'm very easy to please,' he assured her.

'As long as you don't expect something like your mother makes.'

'My mother is a honey but her cooking is a disaster,

I'm relying on you to give her a few tips when you come to Canada.' That was the image to retain in her mind – herself and Sally in Toronto. She held at bay the fear that she might have many periods in the time ahead to fill with trivialities so that the dread that Sally might never come home wouldn't overwhelm her.

In the apartment she brought out a couple of chops and rummaged for salad greens. This was the first meal she had prepared for Rory. She wished it were under happier circumstances.

'Let me make the dressing. It's the only thing I'm expert at,' he offered.

'Who feeds you in Toronto?' she asked.

'I eat lunch at school and generally have a TV snack in the evening,' he told her. 'At weekends I usually go over to my parents for a barbecue – my dad can cook very well. Other members of the family generally drop by too so it ends up as a party.'

'It sounds fun,' she said wistfully.

'You and Sally will have a fine time.'

'You really believe she'll be found safe and well?' Joy turned from the grilling-pan to search his face eagerly. 'I know that I believe it but for me belief is a – a shield against the dark. You do hear of people disappearing for good. Children. One sees pictures in the newspaper years later of some sad-eyed woman telling a reporter that she's never given up hope. I used to think that I'd prefer to know my child was dead than live in such uncertainty, but I was wrong. I really couldn't bear it now if I had final word –' Her voice was shaking. Without moving from the table where he had just set the tossed salad, Rory said,

'You won't get that final word and you won't be living in uncertainty either.'

'The old man – Mr Simon, I mean – he must have seen me take Sally to the cemetery.' Joy put out the chops and sat down, frowning.

'You've thought of something else?' Rory helped her to salad.

'The first time I took her to the cemetery he was already there.'

'Are you sure?' Rory looked at her.

'I'm positive. I remember wondering if it was alright for her to play there and I called –'

She hesitated thinking back to that first chilly spring afternoon. 'I called across to him if it was alright and he just raised a hand and went on trimming the grass verge with a pair of shears. Rory, if he wasn't employed in the cemetery why was he cutting the grass in the first place?'

'Tidying the graves?' Rory was thinking aloud. 'Being a public-spirited citizen? If he didn't follow the pair of you in then he was there for some purpose of his own.'

'Could we –?'

'Hurry up with lunch and go back to the cemetery to take a closer look?'

'Would you mind?'

'If we're going to stick together, you'll have to stop asking foolish questions.' She could have warmed herself at the tenderness in his tone.

'Let's walk there.' She finished what was on her plate and stood up, with no very clear idea of what she had eaten. 'Sally and I walk there and when we reach the gates she runs on ahead. Then I go to the bench and take out my book – oh, Rory, if I'd played with her all the time instead. And I haven't even started to type your manuscript yet.'

'Real life is more important.' He followed her *non sequitur* perfectly. 'You think she may have got into conversation with the old fellow while you were reading?'

'It's the only way it could have happened. When I start reading I'm in another world and though she's not supposed to talk to strangers with me so near she might not have thought.'

'Don't start feeling guilty,' he said. 'That's wasted emotion, you know. Nobody expects you to keep your child on a desert island.'

'I took her there because it was safe from the traffic,' Joy said, brushing a hand across her eyes as they stepped into the street.

'In principle it was a good idea,' he said. 'Come on. If the neighbours catch us visiting the local graveyard again we'll just bare our fangs and ask for Dracula.'

The sun had come out and the cemetery was an oasis of green and gold.

'Where was he cutting the grass when you first saw him?' Rory asked.

'It was ages ago. I've only seen him a few times altogether. Over there somewhere, I think.' She waved a hand vaguely.

'I wondered if he was keeping a particular grave tidy,' Rory said.

'It's an old cemetery. Nobody has been buried here for nearly forty years. You heard what Detective Fuller said that they'll probably concrete it over.'

'There ought to be a register or something, shouldn't there?'

'I suppose so but I don't know where it's kept – how did you find your great-great-aunt Eulalia?'

'Family letter from my great grandfather. It described her funeral and the exact location. I hit on the right grave straightaway.'

'When did she die?'

'Nineteen twenty-nine.'

'If the graves are laid out more or less in chronological order – I mean they started at one end when the first parishioner died and then gradually expanded. But we don't know which one we're looking for.'

'Any grave with Simon on it would probably be the one.' Rory considered for a moment.

'Perhaps we'd better look at each headstone in turn,' Joy said, 'but this place is bigger than it looks.'

'I've nothing else to do today.' Pulling her to him he gave her a quick hard kiss. 'You take the south side and I'll take he north.'

Joy nodded and stepped off the gravel path onto the grass verge where the stones slanted in the tranquil loveliness of the late afternoon. It was peaceful here, soothing her heart despite the anxiety that troubled it. Some of the lettering on the headstones was almost worn away, rubbed smooth by time. There were a few dusty glass domes with yellowing wax flowers beneath. Taste of a bygone age.

Nothing so far. She turned into the second row, bending to read the inscription.

'Joy! Over here!' Rory's voice shattered the silence. He was beckoning her.

She ran, her feet crunching on the gravel. 'Look at that!' Rory sounded triumphant. It was in the middle of the row, neatly lettered.

Here lies Gabriel Simon
1933 – 1943
'Lifted to Peace out of Conflict'
and
Dora Elizabeth Simon nee Gabriel
1910 – 1944
Mother of Gabriel, wife of Nicholas
'Not dead but Passed over.'

'Could Sally read?' Rory asked.

'No, of course not. She's too little. I was teaching her some of the alphabet as a game. Why did you say "could" and not "can"? Are you beginning to think she's –?'

'No,' he said. 'Sorry. This place sends one right back into the past, that's all. Where does she generally play? Which direction?'

'All over. She knows she must keep to the path and the grass verge. Over here – yes, she does play over here sometimes.'

'You can't see this grave from where you usually sit.'

'That's true, but she was always running back to me to tell me how her game was going.'

'But she could have held a fairly long conversation with the old gentleman without your noticing?'

'I suppose so,' Joy looked doubtful. 'Surely she'd have mentioned it to me? She isn't a secretive child.'

'She talked about her friend, Simon, didn't she?'

'Interminably.' The ghost of a smile lifted the edges of her lips. 'After a while I didn't really listen. Rory, I was always so tired, going backwards and forwards to the restaurant. She often chatters and I say the right thing in the appropriate place without really taking any notice.'

'Your guilt-complex is surfacing again,' he warned, putting his arm lightly about her shoulders. 'After a day spent drumming dates into the reluctant heads of my class I find I can't concentrate on what *I'm* saying, let alone anything anyone else comes out with.'

'I used to tell myself that when I wasn't so tired and harassed then I'd make time to play more games, listen more carefully –'

'We have company,' Rory said.

'Great minds think alike,' Detective Fuller said, walking up with Ken on his heels.

'We found what looks like the connection,' Rory said.

'Nicholas Simon.' The detective nodded. 'One of our people spotted that when the cemetery was being checked out during the search. You think he was your caretaker chap?'

'He lost his wife and son,' Joy said.

'Sounds as if the boy died as the result of enemy action and the mother died a year later.' Detective Fuller bent to read the inscription. 'Ken, remind me to commend young Harry for noticing this and recalling it at the right time. Shows initiative. Well, Miss Prentice, it's likely the old boy used to come here to keep the memory of his little family alive.'

'And now he has my daughter.' Her voice was tense.

'Still speculation, but I think we're getting close.' He broke off, turning his head as a soft thud sounded near at hand. Joy, looking in the same direction, felt her heart leap into her throat. Something had been flung over the wall and lay now on the gravel path, its bright blue contrasting with the flint grey of the stones.

'Head him off,' Detective Fuller said sharply as Ken and he began to run. Suddenly everything was happening in a blur of motion. Joy had a confused impression of the policemen going in different directions, of Rory running towards the duffel bag, of his catching at her arm and holding her back as she reached his side.

'Wait!' he said sharply and Joy, staring at the blue canvas, felt the blood drain away from her face as she realised what the bag might contain.

On the other side of the wall the sound of an engine revving up screamed into the summer air. There was another sound too – stuttering, ear-splitting. A motorcycle being ridden too fast. She received no more than an impression of that and then all the sounds merged into a roar, a crashing, a police siren wailing on and on and on –

Somehow she was at the gates without knowing precisely how she had got there. At the corner the police car was stuck out, motionless, its siren wailing. A little further on a motorbike lay on its side, wheels spinning uselessly. A little further – Joy closed her eyes, willing the wave of dizziness to pass.

'Tried to bypass me.' Ken, looking white save where a bruise was already colouring his forehead, was climbing stiffly out of the car. 'Knew I couldn't turn in that narrow space, but he misjudged the distance.'

Detective Fuller was kneeling by the still figure with the helmeted head at an odd angle. When he rose his expression was unhappy. 'Broken neck,' he said succinctly and came back to the stalled police car, leaning in and speaking into the radio. Ken sat down on the seat, mopping his brow gingerly. Time slowed and stopped.

'It was Jimmy Hargreaves, wasn't it?' she said.

'Complete with tattoo.' Detective Fuller had finished his radio message and came over. 'It is an odd thing but he'd the number seventeen on the back of his jacket. Odd how that woman tunes into things. You alright, Ken?'

'I'll live, thank you, sir,' Ken said, standing up again. 'Sorry about that, sir.'

'Not your fault. He tried to do a fast U-turn and came off at the wrong angle. We'd better take a look at the bag – not you, Miss Prentice.'

Now she was inside the gates again, sitting on a bench, her mind empty of everything save a terror so overwhelming that she felt as if she were suffocating.

'Bag's got a couple of rocks in it,' Detective Fuller said loudly, 'and this.' He walked towards her, the slip of paper in his hands. The printing shrieked at her. 'MY APOLOGIES BUT SALLY IS GOING TO FETCH SIMON, SO I MUST KEEP HER.'

'Pity we can't question Hargreaves,' Detective Fuller said.

'But you'll find Nicholas Simon?' Rory's voice was sharp.

'God willing,' Detective Fuller said. He wasn't speaking lightly.

Ten

'Why on a motorcycle?' Joy asked the question with dull despair. 'Why not in the car?'

'He probably figured that by now we'd be aware of the car,' Detective Fuller said. 'We're checking on the bike but it's not a new model. He could have picked it up secondhand.'

'Always checking,' she said. Always talking in that flat, nasal voice that reduced drama and heartbreak to routine. She clenched her fists, fighting back hysteria. They were in the police station again. On the desk were littered mugs in a plastic box. There was a plate with sandwiches on it, their ends curling up slightly. Now and then Detective Fuller took an absent-minded bite out of one. There were other detectives in and out all the time. She supposed that some of them were working on other cases. It wasn't fair to blame anybody for the lack of progress. It wasn't fair that she should have lost Sally.

'Only Hargreaves' prints on the bag apart from your own and Sally's,' he was saying now. 'No prints on the note.'

'Written by the same man?' Rory asked.

'Oh, without a doubt. Miss Prentice, why don't you go home and get some rest?' She shook her head stubbornly. Someone came in with a file. Voices merged in the background. Detective Fuller's voice sharpened.

'Facts on Nicholas Simon,' he said.

'Yes?' She sat bolt upright, her eyes seeming to draw the information out of him.

'Nicholas John Simon. Born 1912 in Marylebone. Married Dora Elizabeth Gabriel in 1932. One son, Gabriel Simon, born 1933. Killed in an air raid in 1943 – they were living in this district then, I presume. Exact address isn't here. Get onto it, Mavis, will you? Check on lists of occupants on bomb-damaged property. Old ARP records might turn up something.'

'And his wife died a year later?'

'Cause of death – tuberculosis. She was only thirty-two.'

'What about Nicholas Simon?' Rory asked. 'Where was he?'

'Probably in the Army. We'll check records but it won't be a quick process.'

'Tomorrow is Sunday,' someone remarked.

'So we all take the day off, is that it?' Joy's voice rose. 'My daughter is in the hands of God knows what but we can't upset the great British Sunday.'

'We'll be working right through,' Detective Fuller said without emphasis.

'Air Force,' Rory said. 'What makes you say that?' Detective Fuller looked at him.

'If he has a walrus moustache then isn't it possible he grew it as a young man? And that sort of moustache was popular in the British Air Force, wasn't it?'

'Among pilots. We'll check.'

That word again. Joy swallowed the words that were rising to meet it and said instead, 'If he was born in 1912 then he'll be drawing an old age pension, won't he?'

'Not necessarily. Some elderly people are quite stubborn about accepting what they persist in regarding as charity from the State, but of course –'

'You'll check,' said Joy and stood up. 'I think I will take that rest now. You'll let me know?'

'The moment we have any useful information at all.'

Walking out with Rory at her side she felt

insubstantial and weak as if her legs were about to float away from beneath her. It was shock, she thought. Shock affected people in different ways. She had never seen a dead body before.

'Do you really mean that – about resting?' Rory was looking at her.

'I'm sick of coming to dead ends,' she said wearily. 'Jimmy Hargreaves could have told us where Sally's being held.'

'But the note proves she's still alive.' He opened the car door, and seemed to change his mind at the last minute about helping her in like an invalid.

'For how long?' Some of her vagueness was dissipated in anger. 'You read that note. Sally is going to fetch Simon. Simon's dead. Gabriel Simon is dead, Rory.'

'Yes, I see.' His face was grave, his tone devoid of false comfort. 'I wish to God that I could think of something brilliant to do.'

She wanted to tell him that she was already grateful for what he had done, for his support, for the beginnings of love between them, but her throat ached with silent weeping.

As they alighted at the apartment block Marie clicked up in her high heels. 'Evening off,' she announced as she joined them. 'Any developments?'

'The police think that Sally is being held by someone called Nicholas Simon whose son was killed during the Second World War,' Rory began.

'Simon? His second name is Simon?' Marie had paled a little.

'The same name as Sally's imaginary friend,' Joy said.

'She must have talked about him to Mr Simon.' Rory said. 'She couldn't have read the inscription on the headstone.'

'But she could,' said Marie.

'What?' Joy stared in her turn.

'It was a few months back. I'd forgotten – you asked me to look in on her one evening. You were busy with customers so I looked in. She was awake and she wanted a story so I took a few minutes off and told her that silly rhyme about Simple Simon and the Pieman. You know the one?'

'And?' Joy had gripped her arm.

'And I printed the name SIMON on my order pad for her, so she would have been able to read it.'

'She must have seen the name on the headstone and recognised it,' Joy said slowly. 'Maybe she spelled it out and Nicholas Simon was cutting the grass nearby and heard her. Could it have happened like that, Rory?'

'I'll never forgive myself,' Marie said starkly.

'It wasn't your fault.' Joy paused to collect her thoughts. 'You told her the rhyme and she invented her friend, Simon. Then she saw the name while she was playing in the cemetery and Nicholas Simon was working nearby. Working unofficially because his wife and son were buried there and nobody was keeping the place very tidy. And he heard Sally and connected her with his dead child – am I describing a crazy person?'

'An obsessed one,' Rory said. 'He's old, going on for eighty now, trying to hang onto the past and the people he loved –'

'Let's not get too sentimental,' Joy said harshly. 'He got Jimmy Hargreaves to steal my daughter and now he's proposing to send her after his son – that's demented, Rory.'

'If I run you to the station can you tell them what you just told us?' Rory asked Marie.

'It will help round out the picture they're building up?' Marie nodded.

'I'm going to lie down before I fall down,' Joy said shiveringly. 'I want to lie down and go through everything in my mind. Not even you there. Please?'

'Do you want me to come by later?'

'May I ring you? If I need you, I mean.'

'Surely.' He kissed her cheek and opened the passenger door for Marie. Joy walked upstairs, consciously keeping her back very straight. Denying the exhaustion that swept over her. There had to be something else to remember, she fretted, as she lay flat on her back, willing sleep to come. Sally had learned to recognise the word Simon, had invented her friend, had seen the name on the headstone – through her mind the scenario was unfolding reel by reel. Sally traced the carved letters on the headstone, pronouncing the name aloud in her clear little voice and the old man cutting the grass had heard her.

And I sat immersed in some novel or other, not even noticing, smug because my child wasn't playing out in the main road where a car might knock her down. Death lives inside the gates of a cemetery, not outside. Not for Sally. Please, God, not for Sally. The police will find Nicholas Simon. Before anything happens.

The pealing of the telephone bell. She must have slept without knowing it. The room was almost dark. She sat up, pushing back her hair, orientating herself from sleep to waking. In the other room she switched on the light as she picked up the receiver.

'Miss Prentice? Detective Fuller here. Hope I didn't disturb you if you were resting.'

'Is there any news?'

'Additional information that I thought you might like to hear as quickly as possible. Your friend told us about the rhyme she'd taught Sally –'

'What news?' she broke in.

'Some results from the checking. Nicholas Simon was a Wing Commander in the Air Force during the Second World War.'

'Wasn't he young for such high rank?' she asked.

'Lord no, not in those days. Most fighter pilots were in their late teens and early twenties. He was already twenty-seven when the war started and he was commissioned immediately.'

'And?' She sat down, gripping the receiver.

'He was decorated. DFC and Bar. A bit of a hero. One among many. His boy, Gabriel, was killed when a bomb demolished the hotel where he and Mrs Simon were staying. Apparently they'd come to spend a weekend leave with Nicholas Simon. The two of them left the boy asleep and popped down to the local pub for a quick drink. That was when the bomb hit. Dora Simon never got over the shock. Spent the next year in a nursing home and just faded away. Nicholas Simon completed his war service and went back to their home in Somerset. The police down there are checking it out now.'

'Where did you learn all this?'

'Contacted his old squadron. Several of them are still alive. We struck lucky and found a couple who recalled the whole business very well. Apparently they regarded him as a bit of a martinet, a stickler for church parades and suchlike. After the war he dropped out of sight. We haven't traced any pension withdrawals yet, but that will be the next step.'

'But we don't have any time,' Joy whispered. 'In the note he said he was sending Sally to bring his son back. Detective Fuller, Gabriel Simon's been dead for forty-five years.'

'Old Mr Simon may have moved back to this area within the last year or so,' his flat voice informed her. 'From what your friend told us he may have heard Sally chattering about Simon, and decided – who knows? Anyway he roped in Jimmy Hargreaves who wasn't too fussy about breaking the law if there was no actual violence involved. Now we're checking from both ends –'

'Do you have his address in Somerset?'

'Peacock Cottage –'

'Peacock?' she interrupted sharply.

'Peacock Cottage, Weare. As far as we've been able to ascertain the place has stood empty for the past year or so, why?'

'Sally told me that Simon's daddy had a peacock. I promised to take her to the zoo – Mr Baird was planning to take us, I wondered where she'd heard the word, but I was in a rush –'

'That would seem to clinch it then. If anything else breaks I'll let you know at once. Now I'm on my way home but there'll be somebody here manning the telephone.'

She said goodbye, replaced the receiver. He was a patient, hard-working man but she had the feeling that time was slipping through her fingers like sand when the tide goes out. Time, something about time. A weekend leave. Dora and Gabriel Simon had come up from Somerset to join Wing Commander Nicholas Simon for a brief reunion. Risking the chance of an air raid. Staying in this district. A direct hit. A bomb-damaged building. An hotel that had been reduced to a pile of rubble in a few minutes. The child had been buried here. Dora Simon had gone into a nursing home. Nicholas Simon had returned to his squadron. The rubble had been cleared away and years later built on again. Built over.

She put her hands up to the sides of her head, balancing the weight of her thoughts. Not in Peacock Cottage – not any longer. Sally wasn't in Somerset. She had to be within sight of the cemetery where that other child was buried.

'Very solid pre-war foundations,' the agent had told her when she moved in. 'Used to be a hotel on this site.'

Her hand reached out to the telephone, hovered and

was withdrawn. No. The police might panic him. She couldn't risk that. A duffel bag flung over the wall, a motor cycle instead of a car; a diversion to occupy the attention of the police while –.

Fear and tiredness fell away like a cloak that had become too heavy. She went into the bathroom and rinsed her face. There was nobody on the staircase. There never had been a watch kept on the apartment block after the first search, the questioning of other tenants. Two apartments on each of the five floors. Directly above her the attics with their empty sacks and packing-cases.

She went noiselessly up the stairs and opened the door at the top. It wasn't even locked. Nobody ever bothered to go up there. In that first instant she saw the shuttered window, the dim lamp burning on the table, the plump little form curled on a heap of sacks.

Nicholas Simon sat at the small table, the old service revolver pointed at her. He must have heard her after all and his voice was calm. 'Come in and close the door, Miss Prentice. I am blessed with abnormally acute hearing for a man of my advanced years. Sally is asleep. A sleeping pill which will wear off in an hour or two. She really isn't hurt. Sit down.'

She sat down on the packing-case he indicated. He occupied a ladder-backed chair behind which the rest of the attics folded themselves away into the darkness.

'Why?' She kept her voice low and conversational. 'Why do you want my child? Gabriel is dead. Sally can't fetch him back.'

'My son is not dead,' he said placidly. 'We none of us really die. The inscription I put on their grave is true though I didn't realise it at the time. Nothing ends. Nobody dies. They pass into a new dimension that can be seen only by the pure in heart. Your little girl can see my son clearly and speak with him. She told me that he has red hair. He did have red hair, like my dear wife.'

'Is that when you decided –?'

'After the war I returned to Peacock Cottage. I had a small private income and I required very little for my physical needs. I waited for them to come home. The years went by –'

'You never remarried?'

'I do not approve of second marriages,' he said reprovingly. 'Dora and I promised each other never to remarry if one of us was taken. I have never broken a promise. I waited. Then it occurred to me that it would be easier to establish contact with them if I were near the place where they were buried. My wife left this world in Somerset but I had her brought here to lie with our child. You know it was my fault in the beginning. "No decent whisky in the hotel bar," I said to Dora. "Let's slip down the road to that pub and see if we can't bribe the bartender to let us have a bottle of the real stuff." Dora was anxious, but I persuaded her. "He won't wake up and he's not a baby." We were only away five minutes and then the Alert sounded and the bomb, following straight afterwards. No time to get back, you see. Fire and noise – you will not have heard a bomb fall? I pray you never will.'

'Where have you been living?'

'A very poky little place about five miles off. I would have taken rooms here but they were all occupied when I enquired. The agent did kindly show me round so I knew the layout – not that I had any thought of using it at that time. I used to visit the cemetery quite often. It was not well maintained. Sloppy, you know. I decided to lend a hand, jolly good exercise at my time of life. That was when I saw Sally.'

'Talking to her imaginary friend, Simon.'

'Talking to my son, Miss Prentice. Pure in heart, you see.'

'Your son's name was Gabriel.'

'He always insisted we called him Simon. Thought Gabriel a soppy name.'

'But why steal her?' Joy asked carefully. Every fibre of her body ached to rush over and pick up the sleeping figure. 'I meant to borrow her for a while,' he said. 'I even considered asking your permission, but then I realised she wasn't being brought up correctly. No father, taken to sleep at the back of a restaurant and then woken up again at midnight. No life for a child.'

'Do you think I don't know that?' A healthy anger bubbled up in her. 'So you hired Jimmy Hargreaves?'

'Rather a wild young man but no real harm in him. We went back to Peacock Cottage for a couple of months. I wished to draw attention away from the apartment block, you see, but I still went to the cemetery often, for the pleasure of seeing Sally.'

'And plan to kidnap her,' Joy said tightly.

'That went splendidly.' His voice sounded like two hands rubbing together. 'Jimmy went to the Sunset and went through to the back to pick up Sally. He couldn't manage her and the teddy bear. I was perturbed about that. When she woke up it was the first thing she asked for.'

'She must have cried for me.'

'Only a little. I explained to her that it was a big game of hide and seek and she settled down quite happily. Of course we couldn't allow her out of the garden but fortunately we have no near neighbours and I kept many of my son's toys. She recognised me from having seen me cutting the grass. I told her as a great secret that I was Simon's daddy so she wasn't afraid. I fear her siren suit is very grubby by now. I do apologise for that.'

'You sent the notes by Jimmy Hargreaves and waited until you thought it safe to sneak back and get in. How did you get in?'

'I drove up from Weare – rather tiring at my age but I parked the car in that rather garish multi-storey car park and then I simply walked through the front door with Sally wrapped in a blanket. You can't afford to have nerves when you're on operations.'

'And nobody would expect the kidnapper to walk in through the front door carrying the child,' Joy said.

'Those stairs are dim even in the daytime and I put the shutters down immediately. Then Jimmy was providing a diversion. A brilliant stroke. I had every confidence in his getting away safely.'

'But he didn't,' Joy said. 'He misjudged his speed and crashed. He's dead.'

There was a brief silence. Then Nicholas Simon said, 'So Jimmy went for a Blighty, did he? I'm sorry about that. He was a good egg.'

'It was an accident.' Joy forced herself to speak quietly. 'Mr Simon, you must let me take Sally now. I don't know what bizarre experiment you had in mind but it won't work.'

'Tonight is the anniversary of his death,' the old man said. 'When Sally wakes up – it is a very mild sleeping pill – she will call my son into manifestation.'

'She will do no such thing.' Joy's voice rose. 'I don't know what you intend but I won't allow you to submit my daughter to any weird experiment. She doesn't talk to your son. Sally's Simon is the Simon of the nursery rhyme. A friend of mine taught her the letters of the name and she recognised them on the headsone. That's all. Your son won't come back and nobody is going to try to fetch him.'

On the heap of sacks Sally wriggled into a sitting position, rubbing sleep out of her eyes. 'Mummy?' The small voice was tentative, and then Joy was kneeling beside her, the long-pent tears pouring down her face.

'Where's teddy?' Sally demanded.

'Oh, Simon's playing with him.' She glanced into the darkness that lay beyond the dim circle of yellowish light cast by the lamp.

'There's nobody there, darling,' Joy said unsteadily. 'Only the teddy. Look.'

She half rose, glimpsing the shape of the fluffy toy, but the revolver had jerked in her direction.

'I'm going to send Sally to fetch my boy,' Nicholas Simon said.

'Simon's playing with the teddy,' Sally said, happily uncomprehending.

'Where's Jimmy?'

'He went to fetch Simon,' Joy said. She had no idea how the words had arisen in her mind, but she let them spill out. 'Jimmy went to fetch him.'

'Not Sally?' The revolver was still pointing in her direction but there was a tremor of uncertainty in the rough old voice. 'It was meant to be Sally.'

'Did your son waste his time playing with three-year-old girls?' Joy demanded. 'Would he have changed so much?' She had Sally by the hand and took a step out of the circle of lamplight.

'Sally is pure of heart.' His voice had strengthened slightly.

'And Jimmy Hargreaves wasn't a real criminal. You said it yourself. A bit wild, you said.'

'Knew plenty like him during the war,' he said. 'Fighting brought out the best in them.'

'And wouldn't your son have followed Jimmy round?' Another cautious step. 'Wanting to know how the car worked, wanting a game of football? He won't come back for Sally. He never did.'

She had almost reached the door. Her hand groped. 'We forgot teddy,' wailed Sally and made a sudden dart across the room just as feet pounded up the stairs.

The revolver wavered wildly.

Joy called out, 'Oh, don't shoot.'

'Nothing to worry about, my dear. All Clear will be sounding in a moment.' Nicholas Simon had risen, the old habit of command strong in his voice. 'Enemy at the ready, Man your gun turrets. I say, chaps, wait for me.'

The bursting open of the door, the firing of the revolver, a chair crashing onto its side merged and melded. Someone grabbed Sally. Arms held her tightly. Rory's arms.

There was a blur of noise, anxious voices, footsteps. She was being supported down the stairs, lowered into an armchair in a room she recognised dimly as her own. Brandy stung her throat and made her eyes water. She wondered who had brought it.

'Darling, are you alright?' That was the first time, she thought in confusion, that he had called her darling.

'Nicholas Simon,' she said chokingly.

'He put the bullet through his own head,' Detective Fuller said.

'Dear God.' Pity and terror shivered through her.

'I guess he finally understood that he couldn't bring his boy back so he went to join him.' Rory said.

'After all these years?' She looked across the room to where Sally sat on Mavis's knee.

'Information was phoned into us from Somerset after I talked with you on the telephone,' Detective Fuller said. 'Lucky they caught me. I was on my way out. Apparently the old fellow has spent the last forty years in and out of various mental homes. After the war he had nothing to sustain the energy that held him together during the war – no more enemy planes to shoot down, no more heroics, only a life without the wife and son for whose deaths he blamed himself. He was discharged as cured about three years ago and took up residence in his old home. And then Mavis here came in to inform me that she'd been doing a little digging into local records and that this apartment block was built over the foundations of an hotel that suffered a direct hit back in 1943. So I doubled back just to check it out.'

'Sally seems to be alright,' Rory said, looking over at her.

'She thought it was all a game,' Joy said.

'I had a holiday,' Sally announced.

'Did he really intend to –?' She couldn't finish the sentence.

'Who can possibly tell what's in the mind of a disturbed old man?' The detective rose, weariness settling over him. 'He was concerned about her welfare and all those notes, his bringing her here in the end, might have been an unconscious cry for someone to find him and stop what he was going to do. I'm no psychologist, only a policeman.'

The police were leaving. She had caught a glimpse of ambulance attendants coming down the stairs before someone closed the door.

Sally was in her lap again, wriggling her warm little body into position, stifling a yawn. Joy hugged her, willing away the reality of nightmare.

'I guess it really is all over bar the shouting,' Rory said. 'We can book your flight to Toronto – if you still feel like taking a chance on a schoolteacher who fancies himself as a novelist.'

'Is it a holiday?' Sally looked up, following the drift.

'Maybe it will be for a lot longer than that,' Joy said, smiling at Rory over her head.

'There'll be real children for you to play with,' Rory told Sally. 'My cousins have kids round about your age. And they have nursery schools there too.'

'Get round the daughter and you have the mother in the palm of your hand,' Joy said. She was still trembling slightly from the stress and shock of those final moments but there was time now to look ahead, to let past events sink gently into the pattern of her life.

'I'd like to play with other kids.' Sally picked up the slang word with relish. 'Simon went with his daddy.'

'Did he, sweetheart?'

'And the lady with red hair,' Sally said. 'One, two, three of them, all together.'

Joy's eyes rested on Rory with a startled questioning look.

'Who knows?' he said gently. 'Who knows?'